"Anthony Horowitz is the lion of children's literature." Michael Morpurgo

"Horowitz has become a writer who converts boys to reading." *The Times*

"A first-class children's novelist." *TES*

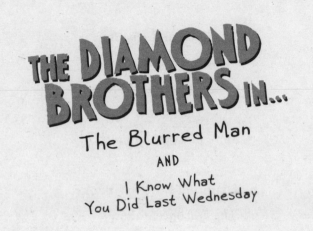

THE DIAMOND BROTHERS IN...

The Blurred Man

AND

I Know What You Did Last Wednesday

**More wickedly funny books
by Anthony Horowitz**

The Devil and His Boy
Groosham Grange
Return to Groosham Grange
The Switch
More Bloody Horowitz

The Diamond Brothers books:
The Falcon's Malteser
Public Enemy Number Two
South by South East
The Blurred Man
The French Confection
I Know What You Did Last Wednesday
The Greek who Stole Christmas

THE DIAMOND BROTHERS IN...

The Blurred Man

AND

I Know What You Did Last Wednesday

ANTHONY HOROWITZ

WALKER
BOOKS

First published individually as *The Blurred Man* (2002) and *I Know What You Did Last Wednesday* (2002) by Walker Books Ltd 87 Vauxhall Walk, London SE11 5HJ

This edition published 2015

2 4 6 8 10 9 7 5 3 1

The Blurred Man, I Know What You Did Last Wednesday © 2002 Gameslayer Ltd Introduction © 2007 Gameslayer Ltd Cover illustrations © 2012 Tony Ross

The right of Anthony Horowitz to be identified as author of this work has been asserted by him in accordance with the Copyright, Designs and Patents Act 1988

This book has been typeset in Sabon

Printed and bound in Great Britain by Clays Ltd, St Ives Plc

British Library Cataloguing in Publication Data: a catalogue record for this book is available from the British Library

ISBN 978-1-4063-6356-2

www.walker.co.uk

CONTENTS

THE BLURRED MAN

I KNOW WHAT YOU DID LAST WEDNESDAY

Dear Reader,

It's been a while since I had lunch with the chairman of Walker Books. He's an old man now. Most of his hair's gone white and the rest of it's just gone. He wears bi-focal glasses but he doesn't really need them. He's forgotten how to read. He'd forget his own name if it wasn't written on his Zimmer frame.

And yet I still remember the day he took me out – just the two of us, face to face, though with a face like his I wouldn't have bothered. We met at the poshest restaurant in London ... then crossed the road to the café on the other side. He ordered two bacon sandwiches without the bacon. He was a vegetarian. And that was when he tried to sweet-talk me into writing an introduction for this collection of stories. But it takes more than a bag of sweets to get Tim Diamond on your side, so I told Walker to take a walk.

A few days later he came tiptoeing round my flat with a bag of books: a bit like Santa Claus without the beard, the laughter or (it was the middle of June) Christmas. This was his deal. Three dozen adventures of Maisy mouse and an old Where's Wally? annual in return for a couple of pages by me. But as far as I was concerned, there was still one book missing. The Walker cheque book ... preferably autographed. Unfortunately, when I pointed this out, the chairman just scowled. That was the sort of man he was: small, hard-edged and leathery. Just like his chair.

"I need an introduction!" he cried.

"All right. How do you do, I'm Tim Diamond," I said.

"No, no, no. For the book!"

"Why do you need an introduction?" Nick – my kid brother – asked. "You probably won't sell any copies anyway."

Actually, in the end, it was Nick who talked me into writing this. He reminded me it's only thanks to Walker that I've become known as England's sharpest, most successful private eye, the sort of detective that makes Hercule Poirot look like a short Belgian with a funny moustache! I have to admit that Walker have been behind me all the way. About thirty miles behind me.

They launched this book with a slap-up dinner at the Ritz. The service was so slow, the waiters deserved to be slapped. Twelve journalists came, but only eleven left. That was how bad the food was.

At the same time, they launched a major advertising campaign ... it's amazing how much you can achieve with three toilet walls and a can of spray paint. Soon the name of Tim Daimond was everywhere. Spelling was never their strong suit. And what can I say about the new covers? They'd been specially designed to stop people noticing the new price. But it was the same old paper though and for that matter the same old stories. They were written so long ago that the Domesday Book was two ahead of them in the bestseller lists, and frankly it had better jokes.

Anyway, here's the introduction. I'm not quite sure how to begin. Introducing the introduction is always the hardest part. I'm glad I'm not a writer. And if you met the guy who does the writing for me, you'd be glad too.

His name is Anthony Horowitz – and I use him to put my adventures down on paper. Let me tell you a bit about him. A lot of people have compared him to JK Rowling. They say he's not as good. He has a wife, two sons, a stuffed dog and a word processor, and the word processor is the only one that doesn't want to leave home. You ever see "Foyle's War", "Midsomer Murders" or "Collision" on TV? Me neither – but he wrote them all. They're the only programmes people fast-forward through to see the advertisements. He also writes a lot of books. About thirty of them at the last count. Enough books to immobilise a mobile library.

I met him just after I'd cracked the case that became known as "The Falcon's Malteser". I don't think his career was doing too well just then. How many other writers tap-dance outside Harrods in their spare time? Anyway, I told him my story, he began to write – and the rest was history. Actually, nobody wanted history. They wanted an adventure. So he had to write it a second time. But it worked. "The Falcon's Malteser" sold twenty-seven copies in Waterstone's the day it was published and I only bought twenty-six of them. Soon we were right at number one in the Bookseller chart. OK – it was the remainders chart but you've got to start somewhere. "The Times" critic said the book was "hysterical" and she should know.

Since then, I've cracked more cases than the entire baggage-handling department at Heathrow Airport, and Horowitz has written them all. "Public Enemy Number Two", "South by South East" – one day maybe he'll come up with a title that somebody actually understands. I had a pretty hairy time in Australia recently and he says that'll come out in a book too. Apparently the title is going to be: "The Radius of the Lost Shark".

Which brings me to the book you are now holding in your hand (unless you didn't buy it, in which case it's still on the shelf ... a bit like my editor).

The two stories in this book all happened to me in the space of one year and all I can say is, I'm glad it wasn't a leap year. One extra day would have been the death of me.

Why do so many people want to kill me? I was nearly shot in "The Blurred Man" and the next time I go on the Millennium Wheel, I want to be sure I'm going to make it the whole way round. There were so many murders in "I Know What You Did Last Wednesday" that it's a miracle I wasn't one of them.

You may have noticed that this edition is printed on special cheap paper and as for the glue ... all I can say is, don't leave it out in the sun. The book is also carbon neutral. A forest in Norway was cut down to produce it but the good news is that another one was planted ... in England. The Norwegians have got too many anyway. You might like to know, ten per cent of every copy sold goes to a very worthwhile charity. Me. I have an overdraft and a hungry kid brother to support.

One last thing. Remember that this book comes with a MONEY BACK GUARANTEE. If for any reason you don't like it, Walker guarantee they won't give you back your money.

All the best,

Tim Diamond

THE
BLURRED
MAN

THE PEN PAL

I knew the American was going to mean trouble, the moment he walked through the door. He only made it on the third attempt. It was eleven o'clock in the morning but clearly he'd been drinking since breakfast – and breakfast had probably come out of a bottle too. The smell of whisky was so strong it made my eyes water. Drunk at eleven o'clock! I didn't like to think what it was doing to him, but if I'd been his liver I'd have been applying for a transplant.

He managed to find a seat and slumped into it. The funny thing was, he was quite smartly dressed: a suit and a tie that looked expensive. I got the feeling straight away that this was someone with money. He was wearing gold-rimmed glasses, and as far as I could tell we were talking real gold. He was about forty years old, with hair that was just turning grey and eyes that were just turning yellow. That must have been the whisky. He took out a cigarette and lit it. Blue smoke filled the room. This man would not have been a good advertisement for the National Health Service.

"My name is Carter," he said at last. He spoke with an American accent. "Joe Carter. I just got in from Chicago. And I've got a problem."

"I can see that," I muttered.

He glanced at me with one eye. The other eye looked somewhere over my shoulder. "Who are you?" he demanded.

"I'm Nick Diamond."

"I don't need a smart-arse kid. I'm looking for a private detective."

"That's him over there," I said, indicating the desk and my big brother, Tim.

"You want a coffee, Mr Carver?" Tim asked.

"It's not Carver. It's Carter. With a 't'," the American growled.

"I'm out of tea. How about a hot chocolate?"

"I don't want a hot anything!" Carter sucked on the cigarette. "I want help. I want to hire you. What do you charge?"

Tim stared. Although it was hard to believe, the American was offering him money. This was something that didn't happen often. Tim hadn't really made any money since he'd worked as a policeman, and even then the police dogs had earned more than him. At least they'd bitten the right man. As a private detective, Tim had been a total calamity. I'd helped him solve one or two cases, but most of the time I was stuck at school. Right now it was the week of half-term – six weeks before Christmas, and once again it didn't look like our stockings were going to be full. Unless you're talking holes. Tim had just seven pence left in his bank account. We'd written a begging letter to our mum and dad in Australia but were still saving up for the stamp.

I coughed and Tim jerked upright in his chair, trying to look businesslike. "You need a private detective?" he said. "Fine. That's me. But it'll cost you fifty pounds a day, plus expenses."

"You take traveller's cheques?"

"That depends on the traveller."

"I don't have cash."

"Traveller's cheques are fine," I said.

Joe Carter pulled out a bundle of blue traveller's cheques, then fumbled for a pen. For a moment I was worried that he'd be too drunk to sign them. But somehow he managed to scribble his name five times on the dotted lines, and slid the cheques across. "All right," he said. "That's five hundred dollars."

"Five hundred dollars!" Tim squeaked. The last time he'd had that much money in his hand he'd been playing Monopoly. "Five hundred dollars...?"

"About three hundred and fifty pounds," I told him.

Carter nodded. "Right. So now let me tell you where I'm coming from."

"I thought you were coming from Chicago," Tim said.

"I mean, let me tell you my problem. I got into England last Tuesday, a little less than a week ago. I'm staying in a hotel in the West End. The Ritz."

"You'd be crackers to stay anywhere else," Tim said.

"Yeah." Carter stubbed his cigarette out in the ashtray. Except we didn't have an ashtray. The smell of burning wood rose from the surface of Tim's desk. "I'm a writer, Mr Diamond. You may have read some of my books."

That was unlikely—unless he wrote children's books. Tim had recently started *Just William* for the fourth time.

"I'm pretty well-known in the States," Carter continued. "*The Big Bullet. Death in the Afternoon. Rivers of Blood*. Those are some of my titles."

"Romances?" Tim asked.

"No. They're crime novels. I'm successful. I make a ton of money out of my writing – but, you know, I believe in sharing it around.

18

I'm not married. I don't have kids. So I give it to charity. All sorts of charities. Mostly back home in the States, of course, but also in other parts of the world."

I wondered if he'd like to make a donation to the bankrupt brothers of dumb detectives, a little charity of my own. But I didn't say anything.

"Now, a couple of years back I heard of a charity operating here in England," he went on. "It was called Dream Time and I kind of liked the sound of it. Dream Time was there to help kids get more out of life. It bought computers and books and special equipment for schools. It also bought schools. It helped train kids who wanted to get into sport. Or who wanted to paint. Or who had never travelled." Carter glanced at me. "How old are you, son?" he asked.

"Fourteen," I said.

"I bet you make wishes sometimes."

"Yes. But unfortunately Tim is still here."

"Dream Time would help you. They make wishes come true." Carter reached into his pocket and took out a hip-flask. He unscrewed it and threw it back. It seemed to do him good. "A little Scotch," he explained.

"I thought you were American," Tim said.

"I gave Dream Time two million dollars of my money because I believed in them!" Carter exclaimed. "Most of all, I believed in the man behind Dream Time. He was a saint. He was a lovely guy. His name was Lenny Smile."

I noticed that Carter was talking about Smile in the past tense. I was beginning to see the way this conversation might be going.

"What can I tell you about Lenny?" Carter went on. "Like me, he never married. He didn't have a big house or a fancy car or anything like that. In fact he lived in a small apartment in a part of London called Battersea. Dream Time had been his idea and he worked for it seven days a week, three hundred and sixty-five days a year. Lenny loved leap years because then he could work three hundred and sixty-six days a year. That was the sort of man he was. When I heard about him, I knew I had to support his work. So I gave him a quarter of a million dollars. And then another quarter. And so on..."

"So what's the problem, Mr Starter?" Tim asked. "You want your money back?"

"Hell, no! Let me explain. I loved this guy Lenny. I felt like I'd known him all my life. But recently, I decided we ought to meet."

"You'd never met him?"

"No. We were pen pals. We exchanged letters. Lots of letters – and e-mails. He used to write to me and I'd write back. That's how I got to know him. But I was busy with my work. And he was busy with his. We never met. We never even spoke. And then, recently,

I suddenly realized I needed a break. I'd been working so hard, I decided to come over to England and have a vacation."

"Wouldn't you have preferred a holiday?" Tim asked.

"I wrote to Lenny and told him I'd like to meet him. He was really pleased to hear from me. He said he wanted to show me all the work he'd been doing. All the children who'd benefited from the money I'd sent. I was really looking forward to the trip. He was going to meet me at Heathrow Airport."

"How would you know what he looked like if you'd never met?" I asked.

Carter blushed. "Well, I did sometimes wonder about that. So once I'd arranged to come I asked him to send me a photograph of himself."

He reached into his jacket and took out a photograph. He handed it to me.

The picture showed a man standing in front of a café in what could have been London or Paris. It was hard to be sure. I could see the words CAFÉ DEBUSSY written on the windows. But the man himself was harder to make out. Whoever had taken the photograph should have asked Dream Time for a new camera. It was completely out of focus. I could just make out a man in a black suit with a full-length coat. He was wearing gloves and a hat. But his face was a blur. He might have had dark hair.

21

I think he was smiling. There was a cat sitting on the pavement between his legs, and the cat was easier to make out than he was.

"It's not a very good picture," I said.

"I know." Carter took it back. "Lenny was a very shy person. He didn't even sign his letters. That's how shy he was. He told me that he didn't like going out very much. You see, there's something else you need to know about him. He was sick. He had this illness ... some kind of allergy."

"Was Algy his doctor?" Tim asked.

"No, no. An allergy. It meant he reacted to things. Peanuts, for example. They made him swell up. And he hated publicity. There have been a couple of stories about him in the newspapers, but he wouldn't give interviews and there were never any photographs. The Queen wanted to knight him, apparently, but sadly he was also allergic to queens. All that mattered to him was his work ... Dream Time ... helping kids. Anyway, meeting him was going to be the biggest moment of my life... I was as excited as a schoolboy."

As excited as a schoolboy? Obviously Carter had never visited my school.

"Only when I got to Heathrow, Lenny wasn't there. He wasn't in London either. I never got to meet him. And you know why?"

I knew why. But I waited for Lenny to tell me.

"Lenny was buried the day before I arrived," Carter said.

"Buried?" Tim exclaimed. "Why?"

"Because it was his funeral, Mr Diamond!" Carter lit another cigarette. "He was dead. And that's why I'm here. I want you to find out what happened."

"What did happen?" I asked.

"Well, like I told you, I arrived here at Heathrow last Tuesday. All I could think about was meeting Lenny Smile, shaking that man's hand and telling him just how much he meant to me. When he didn't show up, I didn't even check into my hotel. I went straight to the offices of Dream Time. And that was when they told me..."

"Who told you?" I asked.

"A man called Hoover. Rodney Hoover..."

"That name sucks," Tim said.

Carter ignored him. "He worked for Lenny, helping him run Dream Time. There's another assistant there too, called Fiona Lee. She's very posh. Upper-class, you know? They have an office just the other side of Battersea Bridge. It's right over the café you saw in that photo. Anyway, it seems that just a few days after I e-mailed Lenny to tell him I was coming, he got killed in a horrible accident, crossing the road."

"He fell down a manhole?" Tim asked.

"No, Mr Diamond. He got run over. Hoover

and Lee actually saw it happen. If they hadn't been there, the police wouldn't even have known it was Lenny."

"Why is that?"

"Because he was run over by a steamroller." Carter shuddered. Tim shivered. Even the desk light flickered. I had to admit, it was a pretty horrible way to go. "He was flattened," the American went on. "They told me that the ambulance people had to fold him before they could get him onto a stretcher. He was buried last week. At Brompton Cemetery, near Fulham."

Brompton. That was where the master criminal known as the Falcon had been buried too. Tim and I had gone to the cemetery at the end of our first ever case*. We were lucky we weren't still there.

"This guy Rodney Hoover tells me he's winding down Dream Time," Carter went on. "He says it wouldn't be the same without Lenny, and he doesn't have the heart to go on without him. I had a long talk with him in his office and I have to tell you ... I didn't like it."

"You don't think it's a nice office?" Tim asked.

"I think something strange is going on."

Tim blinked. "What exactly do you think is strange?"

Carter almost choked on his cigarette. "Goddammit!" he yelled. "You don't think

* See *The Falcon's Malteser*

there's anything unusual in a guy getting run over by a steamroller? It happens in the middle of the night and just a few days before he's due to have a meeting with someone who's given him two million dollars! And the next thing you hear, the charity he'd set up is suddenly shutting down! You don't think that's all a little strange?"

"It's certainly strange that it happened in the middle of the night," Tim agreed. "Why wasn't he in bed?"

"I don't know why he wasn't in bed – but I'll tell you this: I think he was murdered. A man doesn't walk in front of a steamroller. But maybe he's pushed. Maybe this has got something to do with money ... my money. Maybe somebody didn't want us to meet! I know that if I was writing this as a novel, that's the way it would turn out. Anyway, there are plenty of private detectives in London. If you're not interested, I can find someone who is. So are you going to look into this for me or not?"

Tim glanced at the traveller's cheques. He scooped them up. "Don't worry, Mr Carpark," he said. "I'll find the truth. The only question is – where do I find you?"

"I'm still at the Ritz," Carter said. "Ask for Room 8."

"I'll ask for you," Tim said. "But if you're out, I suppose the room-mate will have to do."

*   *   *

25

We changed the traveller's cheques into cash and blew some of it on the first decent meal we'd had in a week. Tim was in a good mood. He even let me have a pudding.

"I can't believe it!" he exclaimed, as the waitress served us two ice-cream sundaes. The service in the restaurant was so slow that they were more like Mondays by the time they arrived. "Three hundred and fifty pounds! That's more money than I've earned in a month."

"It's more money than you've earned in a year," I reminded him.

"And all because some crazy American thinks his pen pal was murdered."

"How do you know he wasn't?"

"Intuition." Tim tapped the side of his nose. "I can't explain it to you, kid. I've just got a feeling."

"You've also got ice-cream on your nose," I said.

After lunch we took the bus over to Fulham. I don't know why Tim decided to start in Brompton Cemetery. Maybe he wanted to visit it for old times' sake. It had been more than a year since we'd last been there, but the place hadn't changed. And why should it have? I doubted any of the residents had complained. None of them would have had the energy to redecorate. The gravestones were as weird as ever, some of them like Victorian telephone boxes, others like miniature castles with doors fastened by rusting chains and padlocks. You'd have needed a skeleton key to open them. The place was divided into separate areas: some old, some more modern. There must have been thousands of people there but of course none of them offered to show us the way to Smile's grave. We had to find it on our own.

It took us about an hour. It was on the edge of the cemetery, overshadowed by the football stadium next door. We might never have found it except that the grave had been recently dug. That was one clue. And there were fresh flowers. That was another. Smile had been given a lot of flowers. In fact, if he hadn't been dead he could have opened a florist's. I read the gravestone:

LENNY SMILE
APRIL 31st 1955 – NOVEMBER 11th 2001
A WONDERFUL MAN, CALLED TO REST.

We stood in silence for a moment. It seemed too bad that someone who had done so much for children all over the world hadn't even made it to fifty. I glanced at the biggest bunch of flowers on the grave. There was a card attached. It was signed in green ink, *With love, from Rodney Hoover and Fiona Lee*.

There was a movement on the other side

of the cemetery. I had thought we were alone when we arrived, but now I realized that there was a man, watching us. He was a long way away, standing behind one of the taller grave-stones, but even at that distance I thought there was something familiar about him, and I found myself shivering without quite knowing why. He was wearing a full-length coat with gloves and a hat. I couldn't make out his face. From this distance, it was just a blur. And that was when I realized. I knew exactly where I'd seen him before. I started forward, running towards him. At that moment he turned round and hurried off, moving away from me.

"Nick!" Tim called out.

I ignored him and ran through the cemetery. There was a gravestone in the way and I jumped over it. Maybe that wasn't a respectful thing to do but I wasn't feeling exactly religious. I reached the main path and sprinted forward. I didn't know if Tim was following me or not. I didn't care.

The northern gates of the cemetery opened onto Old Brompton Road. I burst out and stood there, catching my breath. It came as a shock, coming from the land of the dead into that of the living, with buses and cabs roaring past. An old woman, wrapped in three cardigans, was selling flowers right next to the gate. Business can't have been good. Half the flowers were as dead as the people they were meant for. I went over to her.

"Excuse me..." I said. "Did someone just come out through this gate?"

The old woman shook her head. "No, dear. I didn't see anyone."

"Are you sure? A man in a long coat. He was wearing a hat..."

"People don't come out of the cemetery," the old woman said. "When they get there, they stay there."

A moment later, Tim proved her wrong by appearing at the gate. "What is it, Nick?" he asked.

I looked up and down the pavement. There was nobody in sight. Had I imagined it? No. I was certain. The man I had seen in Joe Carter's photograph had been in the cemetery less than a minute ago. Once I'd spotted him, he had run away.

But that was impossible, wasn't it?

If it was Lenny Smile that I had just seen, then who was buried in the grave?

DEAD MAN'S FOOTSTEPS

We began our search for Lenny Smile the next day – at the Battersea offices of the charity he had created.

I knew the building, of course, from the photograph Carter had shown us. Dream Time's headquarters were above the Café Debussy, which was in the middle of a row of half-derelict shops a few minutes' walk from the River Thames. It was hard to believe that a charity worth millions of pounds could operate from such a small, shabby place. But maybe that was the point. Maybe they didn't want to spend the money they raised on plush offices in the West End. It's the same reason why Oxfam shops always look so run down. That way they can afford another ox.

But the inside of Dream Time was something else. The walls had been knocked through to create an open-plan area with carpets that reached up to your ankles and leather furniture you couldn't believe had started life as a cow. The light fittings looked Italian. Low lighting at high prices. There were framed pictures on the walls, of smiling children from around the world: Asia, Africa, Europe and so on. The receptionist was smiling too. We already knew that the place was being shut down, and I could see that she didn't have a lot to do. She'd just finished polishing her nails when we walked in. While we were waiting she started polishing her teeth.

At last a door opened and Fiona Lee walked in. At least, I guessed it must be her. We'd rung that morning and made an appointment. She was tall and slim, with her dark hair tied back in such a vicious bun that you'd expect it to explode at any moment. She had the looks of a model, but I'm talking the Airfix variety. All plastic. Her make-up was perfect. Her clothes were perfect. Everything about her was perfect, down to the last detail. Either she spent hours getting ready every morning, or she slept hanging in the wardrobe so that she didn't rumple her skin.

"Good morning," she said. Joe Carter had been right about her. She had such a posh accent that when she spoke you heard every letter. "My name is Fiona Lee."

We introduced ourselves.

She looked from Tim to me and back again.

She didn't seem impressed. "Do come in," she said. She spun round on her heel. With heels like hers I was surprised she didn't drill a hole in the floor.

We followed her down a corridor lined with more smiling kids. At the end was a door that led to an office on a corner, with views of Battersea Park one way and the Thames the other. Rodney Hoover was sitting behind a desk cluttered with papers and half-dead potted plants, talking on the telephone. An ugly desk for a very ugly man. Both of them looked like they were made of wood. He was running to fat and might have been a little less fat if he'd taken up running. He had drooping shoulders and jet black hair that oozed oil. He was wearing an old-fashioned suit that was too small for him and glasses that were too big. As he finished his call, I noticed that he had horrible teeth. In fact the last time I'd seen teeth like that, they'd been in a dog. Mrs Lee signalled and we sat down. Hoover hung up. He had been speaking with a strong accent that could have been Russian or German. I noticed he had bad breath. No wonder the potted plants on his desk were wilting.

"Good morning," he said.

"This is Tim Diamond, Mr Hoover," Mrs Lee said. She pronounced his name *Teem Daymond*. "He telephoned this morning."

"Oh yes. Yes!" Hoover turned to Tim. "I

am being sorry that I cannot help you, Mr Diamond." His English was terrible, although his breath was worse. "Right now, you see, Mrs Lee and I are closing down Dream Time, so if you have come about your little brother..."

"I don't need charity," I said.

"We helped a boy like you just a month ago," Fiona Lee said. She blinked, and her eyelashes seemed to wave goodbye. "He had always wanted to climb mountains, but he was afraid of heights."

"So did you buy him a small mountain?" Tim asked.

"No. We got him help from a psychiatrist. Then we paid for him to fly to Mount Everest. That little boy went all the way to the top! And although he unfortunately fell off, he was happy. That is the point of our work, Mr Diamond. We use the money that we raise to make children happy."

"And take the case of Billy!" Hoover added. He pointed at yet another photograph on the wall. If Dream Time had helped many more kids, they'd have run out of wall. "Billy was a boy who wanted to be a dancer. He was being bullied at school. So we hired some bullies to bully the bullies for Billy and now, you see, Billy is in the ballet!"

"Bully for Billy," I muttered.

"So how can we be of helping to you, Mr Diamond?" Hoover asked.

"I have some questions," Tim said. "About a friend of yours called Lenny Smile."

Both Rodney Hoover and Fiona Lee froze. Hoover licked his teeth, which can't have been a lot of fun. Fiona had gone pale. Even her make-up seemed to have lost some of its colour. "Why are you asking questions about Lenny?" she asked.

"Because that way people give me answers," Tim replied. "It's what I do. I'm a private detective."

There was an ugly silence. I had to say that it suited Rodney Hoover.

"Lenny is dead," he said. "You know very well that he's lying there in Brompton Cemetery. Yes? What could you possibly want to know about him?"

"I know he's dead," Tim said. "But I'd be interested to know exactly how he died. I understand you were there."

"We were there," Fiona said. A single tear had appeared in the corner of her eye and began to trickle down her cheek. "Poor, poor Lenny! It was the most ghastly, horrible moment in my life, Mr Diamond."

"I don't suppose it was a terrific moment for him either," I muttered.

She ignored me. "It was about eleven o'clock. Mr Hoover and myself had gone to see him. He didn't like to come out of his flat, so we often went round there to tell him how much money we had raised and how the charity was progressing. We talked. We had a glass of wine. And then we left."

"Lenny said he would come down with us to the car," Hoover continued. "It was a very beautiful night. He wanted to have some of the fresh air ... you know? And so, we left the flat together."

"Lenny was a little bit ahead of us," Fiona Lee explained. "He was a fast walker. Mr Hoover stopped to tie his shoelaces and I waited for him. Lenny stepped into the road. And then..."

"The steamroller was going too fast." He swore quietly in a foreign language. Fiona sighed. "But the driver was on his way home. He was in the hurry. And he ran over Lenny!" He shook his head. "There was nothing, nothing we could do!"

"Do you know the driver's name?" Tim asked.

"I believe it is Krishner. Barry Krishner."

"Do you know what happened to him?"

"He is in a hospital for the hopelessly insane in north London ... in Harrow," Fiona said. "You can imagine that it was a dreadful experience for him, running over a man with a steamroller. But it was his fault! And because he was speeding, he killed one of the most wonderful men who ever lived. Lenny Smile! I had worked for him for twenty years.

35

Mr Hoover too."

"You'd only worked for him for two years?" Tim asked.

"No. I worked with him also for twenty years," Hoover said. "But are you telling me, please, Mr Diamond. Who hired you to ask these questions about Lenny Smile?"

"I never reveal the names of my clients," Tim replied. "Joe Carter wants to remain anonymous."

"Carter!" Hoover muttered. He gave Tim an ugly look. It wasn't difficult. "I could have guessed this. Yes! He came here, asking all his questions as if Fiona and me..." He stopped himself. "There was not one thing suspicious about his death, Mr Diamond. It was an accident. We know. Why? Because we were there! You think someone killed him? Poppycock! Who would wish to kill him?"

"Maybe he had enemies," Tim said.

"Everybody loved Lenny," Fiona retorted. "Even his enemies loved him. All he did his whole life was give away money and help young people. That man built so many orphanages, we had to advertise for orphans to fill them."

"What else can you tell us about him?" I asked.

"It's hard to describe Lenny to someone who never met him."

"Try. Where did he live?"

"He rented a flat in Welles Road. Number seventeen. He didn't buy anywhere because he hated spending money on himself." She took out a tiny handkerchief and dabbed the corner of her eye. "It is true that he liked to be on his own a lot."

"Why?"

"Because of his allergies."

I remembered now. Carter had said he was sick.

"What was he allergic to?" I asked.

"Many, many things," Hoover replied. "Chocolate, peanuts, yoghurt, animals, elastic bands, insects..."

"If he was stung by a wasp, he would be in hospital for a week," Fiona agreed.

"He was also allergic to hospitals. He had to go to a private clinic." Hoover stood up. Suddenly the interview was over. "Lenny Smile was a very unique man. He was – as you say – one in a million. And you have no right ... no right to come here like this. You are wrong! Wrong with all your suspiciousness."

"Yes." Fiona nodded in agreement. "His death was a terrible accident. But the police investigated. They found nothing. Mr Hoover and I were there and we saw nothing."

"You can say to your 'anonymous' client, Mr Carter, that he should go back to Chicago," Hoover concluded. "And now, please, I think you should leave."

We left. The last thing I saw was Rodney Hoover standing next to Fiona Lee. The two of them were holding hands. Were they just co-workers, friends … or something more? And there was something else. Hoover had said something. I wasn't sure what it was, but I was certain he had told me something that in fact he didn't want me to know. I tried to play back the conversation but it wouldn't come.

Tim and I left the offices of Dream Time together. Rodney Hoover and Fiona Lee had given us both the creeps. Neither of us said anything. But we both looked very carefully before we crossed the road.

At least Fiona had given us Smile's address, and as it wasn't far away that was where we went next.

Welles Road was round the back of Battersea, not far from the famous dogs' home. The tall, red-bricked buildings were all mansion flats … not as big as mansions, but certainly smarter than your average flat. There were a dozen people living in each block, with their names listed on the front door. It turned out that Smile had lived at 17A – on the fifth floor. We rang the bell, but there was no answer so we tried 17B. There was a pause, then a woman's voice crackled over the intercom.

"Who is it?"

"We're friends of Lenny Smile," I shouted

back before Tim could come up with a story of his own.

"The fifth floor!" the voice called out. There was a buzz and the door opened.

With its faded wallpaper and worn carpets, the building seemed somehow tired inside. And so were we by the time we got to the fifth floor. The lift wasn't working. The whole place smelled of damp and yesterday's cooking. I thought you needed to be rich to live in Battersea (unless, of course, you happened to be a dog). But anyone could have lived here if they weren't fussy. The fifth floor was also the top floor. The door of 17B was open when we arrived.

"Mr Smile is dead!"

The woman who had broken the news to us so discreetly was about eighty, with white hair that might have been a wig and a face that had long ago given up trying to look human. Her eyes, nose and mouth all seemed to have run into each other like a melting candle. Her voice was still crackling, even without the intercom system. She was dressed in a pale orange dress decorated with flowers; the sort of material that would have looked better on a chair. There were fluffy pink slippers on her feet. Her legs – what I could see of them – were stout and hairy and made me glad that I couldn't see more.

"Who are you?" Tim asked.

39

"My name's Lovely."

"I'm sure it is," Tim agreed. "But what is it?"

"I just told you, dear. Lovely! Rita Lovely! I live next door to Mr Smile. Or at least ... I used to."

"Have you moved?" Tim asked.

Mrs Lovely blinked at him. "No. Don't be daft! Mr Smile is the one who's moved. All the way to Brompton Cemetery!"

"We know that," Tim said. "We've already been there."

"Then what do you want?"

"We want to get into his flat."

"Why?"

I decided it was time to take over. "Mr Smile was my hero," I lied. I'd put on the little-boy-lost look that usually worked with very old women. And also, for that matter, with Tim. "He helped me."

"He gave you money?" She looked at me suspiciously.

"He saved my life. I had a rare disease."

"What disease?"

"It was so rare, it didn't have a name. Mr Smile paid for my medicine. I never got a chance to thank him. And I thought, if I could at least see where he lived..."

That softened her. "I've got a key," she said, taking it out of her pocket. "I was his neighbour for seven years and I used to look after the place for him when he was away. You seem a nice boy, so I'll let you in, just for a few minutes. This way…"

It seemed to take her for ever to reach the door, but then she was very old. At last we were in. Mrs Lovely closed the door behind us and sat down to have a rest.

Smile's flat was small and ordinary. There was a living-room, but it was so neat and impersonal that it was hard to believe anyone had done any living there at all. There was a three-piece suite, a coffee table, a few ornaments. The pictures on the wall were even less interesting than the walls they hung on. It was the same story in the other rooms. The flat told us nothing about the person who had lived there. Even the fridge was empty.

"How often did you see Mr Smile?" I asked.

"I never saw him," Tim replied.

"I know, Tim. I'm asking Mrs Lovely."

"I hardly ever saw him," Mrs Lovely said. "He kept himself to himself, if you want the truth. Although I was here the night that he got run over."

"Did you see what happened?"

"Not really, no." She shook her head vigorously and then readjusted her hair and teeth. "But I did see him go out. There were two people with him, talking to him. They seemed to be helping him down the stairs."

"Helping him?"

41

"One on each side of him. A man and a woman..."

That would have been Rodney Hoover and Fiona Lee.

"After they'd gone, I heard the most terrible noise. It was a sort of rumble and then a scrunching. At first I thought it was my indigestion, but then I looked out of the window. And there they were! The two of them and the driver—"

"Barry Krishner..."

"I don't know his name, young man. But yes, the driver of the steamroller was there. He was looking as sick as a parrot. Hardly surprising!"

"What happened to the parrot?" Tim asked.

"There was no parrot!"

"You mean ... it got so sick it died?"

"There was the driver, the two people I had seen on the stairs and blood all over the road!" Mrs Lovely sighed. "It was the worst thing I have ever seen, and I've lived through two world wars! Blood everywhere! Lots and lots and lots of blood..."

"Thank you," Tim interrupted, going pale.

"Were there no other witnesses?" I asked.

"Just one." Mrs Lovely leant forward. "There was a balloon-seller on the other side of the road. He must have seen everything. I've already been asked about him once, so before you ask me again let me tell you that

I don't know his name or where he had come from. He was an old man. He had a beard and about fifty helium balloons. Floating above his head."

"Why was his beard floating over his head?" Tim asked.

"The balloons, Tim!" I growled. I turned to Mrs Lovely. "Is there anything else you can tell us?" I asked. "Anything about Lenny Smile?"

"No. Not really." Suddenly there were tears in the old woman's eyes. She took out a handkerchief and blew her nose loudly. "I will miss him. It's true I hardly ever saw him, but he was a gentleman. Look at this note he sent me. It was my ninety-first birthday last week and he slipped it under the door."

She produced a crumpled sheet of paper, torn out of an exercise book. There were a couple of lines written in green ink:

Dear Mrs Lovely,
I hope you have a lovely birthday.
L.S.

That was all. The note couldn't have been less interesting or informative. And yet even so I thought there was something strange about it, something that didn't quite add up. I handed it back.

"Nobody else remembered my birthday," Mrs Lovely sighed. "I didn't get any cards. But then, most of my friends were blown up in the war..." She wiped her eyes. "I couldn't have asked for a more quiet neighbour," she said. "And now that he's gone, I'll really miss him."

How could she miss him when she had hardly ever met him? And why had Lenny Smile taken so much care not to be seen? I was beginning to realize that it wasn't just Carter's photograph that had been blurred. The same thing could be said for everything in Lenny Smile's life.

We found Barry Krishner, the steamroller driver, easily enough. There was only one institute for the hopelessly insane in Harrow. Well, two if you count the famous public school which was just a little further down the road. The hospital was a big, Victorian building, set in its own grounds with a path leading up to the front door.

"Are you sure this is the right place?" Tim asked.

"Yes," I said. "They've even got crazy paving."

I have to say, I was a bit worried about going into a mental asylum with Tim. I wondered if they'd let him out again. But it was too late to back out now. One of the doctors, a man called Eams, was waiting for us at the entrance. He was a short man, bald with a little beard that could have been bought at a joke shop. We introduced ourselves and he led us out of the winter sunlight into the gloomy heart of the building.

"Krishner has responded very well to treatment," he said. "Otherwise I would not let you speak with him. Even so, I must ask you to be extremely careful. As I am sure you can imagine, running someone over with a steamroller would be a very upsetting experience."

"For Lenny Smile?" Tim asked.

"For the driver! When Krishner first came here, he was in a state of shock. He ate very little. He barely spoke. Every night he woke up screaming."

"Bad dreams, Dr Eams?" Tim asked.

"Yes. But we have given him a lot of therapy and there has been considerable improvement. However, please, Mr Diamond, try not to refer to what happened. Don't mention any of the details – the steamroller, the accident itself. You have to be discreet!"

"Discreet is my middle name!" Tim nodded.

"And also please bear in mind, he is not a lunatic. He is here as my patient. So don't say anything that would make him think he is mentally ill."

Tim laughed. "I'd be mad to do that!" He nudged the doctor. "So, where's his padded cell?"

Barry Krishner was sitting in a small, old-fashioned room that could just as easily have belonged to a seaside hotel as an asylum. A large window looked out onto the garden and there were no bars. He was a small, grey-haired man, dressed in an old sports jacket and dark trousers. I noticed his eyes blinked a lot behind his spectacles, and he kept on picking his nails. Otherwise it would have been impossible to tell that he had, until recently, been in shock.

"Good afternoon, Barry," Dr Eams said. "These people want to ask you some very important questions about Lenny Smile." Krishner twitched as if he had just been electrocuted. Dr Eams smiled and continued in a soothing tone of voice. "You have nothing to worry about. They're not going to upset you." He nodded at Tim.

"It must have been a crushing experience," Tim began.

Krishner whimpered and twisted in his chair. Dr Eams frowned at Tim, then gently took hold of Krishner's arm. "Are you all right, Barry?" he asked. "Would you like me to get you a drink?"

"Good idea," Tim agreed. "Why not have a squash?"

Krishner shrieked. His glasses had slipped off his nose and one of his eyes had gone bloodshot.

"Mr Diamond!" Eams was angry now. "Please could you be careful what you say. You

46

told me you were going to ask Barry what he saw outside Lenny Smile's house."

"Flat," Tim corrected him.

Krishner went completely white. I thought he was going to pass out.

Dr Eams stared at Tim. "For heaven's sake...!" he rasped.

"OK, doc." Tim winked. "I think it's time we got to the crunch..."

Krishner began to foam at the mouth.

"I really want to crack this case. Although I have to say, the clues are a bit thin on the ground..."

Barry Krishner screamed and jumped out of the window. Without opening it. Alarms went off all over the hospital and, two minutes later, Tim and I were being escorted off the premises with the gates locked securely behind us.

"They weren't very helpful," Tim muttered. "Do you think it was something I said?"

I didn't answer. We had spent the whole day following in a supposedly dead man's footsteps. They had led us nowhere.

So where did we go now?

A NIGHT
AT THE CIRCUS

The next day was a Saturday. Tim was in a bad mood when he came in for breakfast. He'd obviously got out of bed the wrong side: not a good idea, since he slept next to the window. At least there was food in the fridge. The money that Joe Carter had paid us would last us a month, and that morning I'd cooked up eggs, bacon, tomatoes, sausages and beans. The papers had arrived – the *Sun* for me, the *Dandy* for Tim. An hour later the two of us were so full we could barely move. There's nothing like a great British breakfast for a great British heart attack.

But the truth is, we were both down in the dumps – and this time I don't mean the flat. We were no nearer to finding the truth about Smile. Rodney Hoover and Fiona Lee, the pair who ran Dream Time, were obviously creepy. According to Mrs Lovely, the next-door neighbour, they had half-carried Smile downstairs just before his fatal accident. Had he been drunk? Or drugged? They could have thrown him in front of the steamroller – but if so, why? As Tim would doubtless have said, they'd have needed a pressing reason.

Barry Krishner, the driver of the steamroller, hadn't been able to tell us anything. After his encounter with Tim, it would probably be years before he talked again. He might babble and jibber, but I guessed talking would be a little beyond him. The police had presumably investigated and found nothing. Maybe there was nothing to find.

And yet...

Part of me still wondered if Lenny Smile really was dead. I remembered the man I had glimpsed in Brompton Cemetery. He had looked remarkably like the man I had seen in the photograph, and had certainly taken off fast enough when I spotted him. But if Lenny wasn't dead, where was he? And who was it who had disappeared under the steamroller?

"I give up!" Tim exclaimed.

He seemed to be reading my mind. "This isn't an easy case," I agreed.

"No!" He pointed. "I'm talking about this crossword in the *Dandy!*"

I ignored him and flicked over the page in my newspaper. And that was when I saw it. It was on the same page as the horoscopes. An advertisement for a circus in Battersea Park.

Direct from Moscow
THE RUSSIAN STATE CIRCUS
Starring
The Flying Karamazov Brothers
Karl "On Your" Marx – The Human Cannon-ball
The Fabulous Tina Trotsky
Three Sisters on Unicycles
And much, much more!

There was a picture showing a big top, but it was what was in front that had caught my eye. It was a figure in silhouette. A man selling balloons.

"Look at this, Tim!" I exclaimed, sliding the newspaper towards him.

Tim quickly read the page. "That's amazing!" he said. "I'm going to meet an old friend!"

"What are you talking about?"

"My horoscope. That's what it says…"

"Not the horoscopes, Tim! Look at the advertisement underneath!"

Tim read it. "This is no time to be going to the circus, Nick," he said. "We're on a case!"

"But look at the balloon-seller!" I took a deep breath. "Don't you remember what Mrs Lovely said? There was a witness when Lenny Smile was killed. It was a man selling balloons. I thought that was odd at the time.

Why should there have been a balloon-seller in Battersea Park in the middle of the night?"

"He could have been lost…"

"I don't think so. I think he must have been part of the circus. There's a picture of him here in the paper. Maybe the balloon-seller was advertising the circus!"

"You mean … on his balloons?"

"Brilliant, Tim! Got it in one."

Tim ripped the page of the newspaper in half. He must have accidentally caught hold of the tablecloth, because he ripped that in half too. He folded the paper into his top pocket. "It's your turn to do the washing-up," he said. "Then let's go!"

In fact we didn't go back to Battersea until that evening. According to the advertisement, there was only one performance of the circus that day – at seven thirty – and I didn't see any point in turning up before. If the balloon-seller really was part of the big top, he'd probably be somewhere around during the performance. We would catch up with him then.

I don't know what you think about circuses. To be honest, I've never been a big fan. When you really think about it, is there anybody in the world less funny than a clown? And what can you say about somebody who has spent half their life learning how to balance thirty spinning plates and an umbrella on their nose?

51

OK. It's clever. But there simply have to be more useful things to do with your time! And, for that matter, with your nose. There was a time when they used to have animals – lions and elephants – performing in the ring. They were banned and I have to agree that was a good idea. But for my money they could ban the rest of the performers too, and put everyone out of their misery. I'm sorry. I've heard of people who have run away to join a circus, but speaking personally I'd run away to avoid seeing one.

But that said, I had to admit that the Russian State Circus looked interesting. It had parked its tent right in the middle of the park and there was something crazy and old-fashioned about the bright colours and the fluttering flags all edged silver by a perfect November moon. Four or five hundred people had turned out to see the show, and there were stilt-walkers and jugglers keeping the lines amused as they queued up to get in. As well as the tent itself there were about a dozen caravans parked on the grass, forming a miniature town. Some of these were modern and ugly. But there were also wooden caravans, painted red, blue and gold, that made me think of Russian gypsies and Russian palm-readers – old crones telling your future by candlelight. Tim had had his palm read once, when we were in Torquay. The palm-reader had laughed so much she'd had to lie down ... and that was only the contents of one finger on his left hand.

We bought tickets for the show. Tim wanted to see it, and having come all this way across London, I thought why not? We bought two of the last seats and followed the crowd in. Somehow the tent seemed even bigger inside than out. It was lit by flaming torches on striped, wooden poles. Grey smoke coiled in the air and dark shadows flickered across the ring. The whole place was bathed in a strange, red glow that seemed to transport us back to another century. The top of the tent was a tangle of ropes and wires, of rings and trapezes, all promises of things to come, but right now the ring was empty. There were wooden benches raked up in a steep bank, seven rows deep, forming a circle all round the sawdust. We were in the cheapest seats, one row from the back. As a treat, I'd bought Tim a stick of candyfloss. By the time the show started, he'd managed to get it all over himself as well as about half a dozen people on either side.

A band took its place on the far side of the ring. There were five players, dressed in old, shabby tailcoats. They had faces to match. The conductor looked about a hundred years old. I just hoped the music wouldn't get too exciting – I doubted his heart would stand it. With a trembling hand, he raised his baton and the band began to play. Unfortunately, the players all began at different times and what followed was a tremendous wailing and screeching as they all raced to get to the end first. But the conductor didn't seem to notice and the audience loved it. They'd come out for a good time and even when the violinist fell off his chair and the trombonist dropped his trombone they cheered and applauded.

By now I was almost looking forward to seeing the show ... but as things turned out, we weren't going to see anything of the performance that night.

The band came to the end of its first piece and began its second – which could have been either a new piece or the same piece played again. It was hard to be sure. I was glancing at the audience when suddenly I froze. There was a man sitting in the front row, right next to the gap in the tent where the performers would come in. He was wearing a dark coat, a hat and gloves. He was too far away. Or maybe it was the poor light or the smoke. But once again his face was blurred. Even so, I knew him at once.

It was the man from the Brompton Cemetery.

The man in the photograph at the Café Debussy.

Lenny Smile!

I grabbed hold of Tim. "Quick!" I exclaimed.

"What is it?" Tim jerked away, propelling the rest of his candyfloss off the end of his stick and into the lap of the woman behind him.

"There!" I pointed. But even as I searched for Lenny across the crowded circus, I saw him get up and slip out into the night. By the time Tim had followed my finger to the other side of the tent, he had gone.

"Is it a clown?" Tim asked.

"No, Tim! It's the blurred man!"

"Who?"

"Never mind. We've got to go…"

"But the circus hasn't even begun!"

I dragged Tim to his feet and we made our way to the end of the row and out of the big top. My mind was racing. I still didn't know who the man in the dark coat really was. But if it was the same person I had seen at the cemetery, what was he doing here? Could he perhaps have followed us? No – that was impossible. I was sure he hadn't seen us across the crowded auditorium. He was here for another reason, and somehow I knew it had nothing to do with spinning plates and custard pies.

We left the tent just as the ringmaster, a tall man in a bright red jacket and black top hat, arrived to introduce the show. I heard him bark out a few words in Russian, but by then Tim and I were in the open air with the moon high above us, the park eerie and empty and the caravans clustered together about thirty metres away.

"What is it?" Tim demanded. He had forgotten why we had come and was disappointed to be missing the show.

Quickly I told him what I had seen. "We've got to look for him!" I said.

"But we don't know where he is!"

"That's why we've got to look for him."

There seemed to be only one place he could have gone. We went over to the caravans, suddenly aware how cold and quiet it was out here, away from the crowds. The first caravan was empty. The second contained a dwarf sipping sadly at a bottle of vodka. As we made our way over to the third, a man dressed in a fake leopard skin walked past carrying a steel girder. Inside the tent I heard the ringmaster come to the end of a sentence and there was a round of applause. Either he had cracked a joke or the audience was just grateful he'd stopped talking. There was a drum roll. We approached the fourth caravan.

Lenny Smile – if that's who it was – had disappeared. But there was another dead man in Battersea Park that night.

I saw the balloons first and knew at once whose caravan this was. There were more than fifty of them, every colour imaginable, clinging together as if they were somehow alive and knew what had just happened. The strange thing was that they did almost seem to be cowering in the corner. They weren't touching the ground. But the balloon-seller was. He was stretched out on the carpet with something silver lying next to his outstretched hand.

"Don't touch it, Tim!" I warned.

Too late. Tim had already leaned over and picked it up.

It was a knife. The blade was about ten centimetres long. It matched, perfectly, the ten-centimetre deep wound in the back of the balloon-seller's head. There wasn't a lot of blood. The balloon-seller had been an old man. Killing him had been like attacking a scarecrow.

And then somebody screamed.

I spun round. There was a little girl there in a gold dress with sequins. She was sitting on a bicycle which had only one wheel, pedalling back and forth to stop herself falling over. She was pointing at Tim, her finger trembling, her eyes filled with horror, and suddenly I was aware of the other performers appearing, coming out of their caravans as if this was the morning and they'd just woken up. Only it was the middle of the night and these people weren't dressed for bed! There was a clown in striped pants with a bowler hat and (inevitably) a red nose. There was a man on stilts. A fat man with a crash helmet. Two more sisters on unicycles. The strong man had come back with his steel girder. A pair of identical twins stood like mirror images, identical expressions on their faces. And what they were all looking at was my big brother Tim, holding a knife and hovering in the doorway of a man who had just been murdered.

The little girl who had started it screamed once more and shouted something out. The strong man spoke. Then the clown. It all came out as jibberish to me but it didn't take a lot of imagination to work out what they were saying.

"Boris the balloon man has been murdered!"

"Dear old Boris! Who did it?"

"It must have been the idiotic-looking Englishman holding the knife."

I don't know at what precise moment the mood turned nasty, but suddenly I realized that the people all around me no longer wanted to entertain us. The clown stepped forward and his face was twisted and ugly ... as well as being painted white with green diamonds over his eyes. He asked Tim something, his voice cracking with emotion and his make-up doing much the same.

"I don't speak Russian," Tim said.

"You kill Boris!"

So the balloon man really was called Boris. The clown was speaking English with an incredibly thick accent, struggling to make himself understood.

"Me?" Tim smiled and innocently raised a hand. Unfortunately it was the hand that was still holding the knife.

"Why you kill Boris?"

"Actually, I think you mean 'why *did* you kill Boris,'" Tim corrected him. "You've forgotten the verb..."

"I don't think they want an English lesson, Tim," I said.

Tim ignored me. "I kill Boris, you kill Boris, he killed Boris!" he explained to the increasingly puzzled clown.

"I didn't kill Boris!" I exclaimed.

"They killed Boris!" the clown said.

"That's right!" Tim smiled encouragingly.

"No, we didn't!" I yelled.

It was too late. The circus performers were getting closer by the second. I didn't like the way they were looking at us. And there were more of them now. Four muscle-bound brothers in white leotards had stepped out of the shadows. The ringmaster was staring at us from the edge of the tent. I wondered who was entertaining the audience. The entire circus seemed to have congregated outside.

The ringmaster snapped out a brief command in Russian.

"Let's go, Tim!" I said.

Tim dropped the knife and we turned and fled just as the performers started towards us. As far as they were concerned, Tim had just murdered one of their number, and this was a case of an eye for an eye – or a knife wound for a knife wound. These were travelling performers.

They had their own rules and to hell with the country in which they found themselves.

Tim and I took off across the park, trying to lose ourselves in the shadows. Not easy with a full moon that night. Something huge and solid sailed across the sky, then buried itself in the soft earth. The strong man had thrown his girder in our direction. We were lucky – he was strong, but he obviously had lousy aim. The girder would be found the next day sticking out of the grass like a bizarre, iron tree. Half a metre to the right and we'd have been found underneath it.

But I quickly realized that this was only the start of our troubles. The entire circus troupe had abandoned the performance in order to come after us. Word had quickly got round. We had killed old Boris and now they were going to kill us. There was a dull *whoomph!* and a figure shot through the air. It was the man in the crash helmet. This had to be Karl "On Your" Marx, the human cannon-ball. They had fired him in our direction, and I just had time to glimpse his outstretched fists as he soared through the night sky before I grabbed hold of Tim and threw him onto the grass. Marx whizzed past. We had been standing in front of an oak tree and there was a dull crunch as he hit the trunk, ending up wedged in a fork in the branches.

"Do you think he's OK?" Tim asked.

"I don't think he's oak anything!" I replied. "Come on!"

We scrabbled to our feet just as the clown set off across the grass, speeding towards us in a tiny, multicoloured car. I looked ahead with a sinking heart. We really were in the middle of nowhere, with grass all around, the river in the far distance and nobody else in sight. Anybody who had come to the park at that time of night would now be in the circus, watching the show.

"Run, Tim!" I gasped.

The clown was getting nearer. I could see his face, even less funny than usual, the grease paint livid in the moonlight. In seconds he would catch up with us and run us down. But then there was an explosion. The bonnet of the car blew open, the wheels fell off, water jetted off the radiator and smoke billowed out of the boot. The clown must have pressed the wrong button. Either that, or the car had done what it was designed for.

"Which way?" Tim panted.

I turned and looked back. For a brief, happy moment, I thought we had left the circus folk behind us, but then something whizzed through the darkness and slammed into the bark of another tree. It was a knife – but thrown from where? I looked up. There was a long telephone wire crossing the park, connected to a series of poles. And, impossibly, a man was standing, ten metres above the ground, reaching for a second knife. It was a tightrope walker. He had followed us along the telephone wires and was there now, balancing effortlessly in mid-air. At the same time, I heard the sudden cough of an engine and saw a motorbike lurch across the lawn. It was being driven by one of the brothers in white leotards. He had two more brothers standing on his shoulders. The fourth brother was on top of the other two brothers, holding what looked horribly like an automatic machine-gun. The motorbike rumbled towards us, moving slowly because of the weight of the passengers. But as I watched, it was overtaken by the three sisters on their unicycles. The moonlight sparkled not only on their sequins but on the huge swords which one of the other performers must have given them. All three of them were yelling in high-pitched voices, and somehow I knew that I wasn't hearing a Russian folk song. The man on stilts came striding towards us, moving like some monstrous insect, throwing impossibly long shadows across the grass. Somehow he had got ahead of us. And finally, to my astonishment, there was a sudden bellow and a full-sized adult elephant came lumbering out of the trees with a girl in white feathers sitting astride its neck. This would have to be the lovely Tina Trotsky. And despite the law, the Russian State Circus did have an animal or two hidden in its big top.

They had an elephant! Did they also, I wondered, have lions?

Tim had seen it too. "They've got an elephant!" he exclaimed.

"I've seen it, Tim!"

"Is it African or Indian?"

"What?"

"I can never remember which is which!"

"What does it matter?" I almost screamed the words. "It won't make any difference when it stamps on us!"

The circus performers were closing in on us from all sides. There was a rattle from the machine-gun and bullets tore into the ground, ripping up the grass. The dwarf I had seen in the caravan had woken up. It now turned out he was a fire-eating dwarf ... at least, that might explain the flame-thrower he had strapped to his back. We had the elephant, the motorbike and the unicycles on one side. The dwarf and the stilt man were on the other. The tightrope walker was still somewhere overhead. The human cannon-ball was disentangling himself from the tree.

Things weren't looking good.

But then a car suddenly appeared, speeding across the grass. It raced past one of the unicyclists, knocking her out of the way, then curved round, snapping the stilt man's stilts in half. The stilt man yelled and dived head first into a bank of nettles. The elephant fell back, rearing up. Tina Trotsky somersaulted backwards, feathers fluttering all around her. The car skidded to a halt next to us and a door swung open.

"Get in!" someone said, and already I knew that I recognized the voice.

"Are you a taxi?" Tim asked. I think he was worrying about the fare.

"It doesn't matter what it is, Tim," I said. "Just get in!"

I pushed Tim ahead of me and dived onto the back seat. There was another rattle of machine-gun fire, a burst of flame and a loud thud as a second knife slammed into the side of the door. But then the car was moving, bouncing up and down along the grass. I saw a bush blocking the way, right in front of us. The driver went straight through it. There was a road on the other side. A van swerved to avoid us as our tyres hit concrete, and a bus swerved to avoid the van. I heard the screech of tyres and the even louder screech of the drivers. There was the sound of crumpling metal. A horn blared.

But then we were away, leaving Battersea Park far behind us.

It's like I said. I'd never liked the circus. And the events of the night had done nothing to change my mind.

THE REAL
LENNY SMILE

"Well, well, well. This is a very nasty surprise. The Diamond brothers! Having a night at the circus?"

It was the driver of the car, the man who had saved us, who was speaking. He had driven us directly to his office at New Scotland Yard. It had been a while since we had last seen Detective Chief Inspector Snape. But here he was, as large as life and much less enjoyable.

It had been Snape who had once employed Tim as a police-constable. He had been no more than an inspector then – and he'd probably had far fewer grey hairs. He was a big, solid man who obviously worked out in a gym. Nobody got born with muscles like his. He had small blue eyes and skin the colour of raw ham. He was wearing a made-to-measure suit but unfortunately it had been made to measure somebody else. It looked as if it was about to burst. His tie was crooked. So were his teeth. So were most of the people he met.

I had never known his name was Freddy but that was what was written on the door. He had an office on the fourth floor, overlooking the famous revolving sign. I had been involved with Snape twice before: once when we were on the trail of the Falcon, and once when he had forced me to share a cell with the master criminal, Johnny Powers*. He wasn't someone I'd been looking forward to meeting a third time – even if he had just rescued us from the murderous crowd at the Russian State Circus.

His assistant was with him. Detective Superintendent Boyle hadn't changed much since the last time I'd seen him either. *His* first name must have been "Push". That was what was written on his door. Short and fat with curly black hair, he'd have done well in one of those BBC documentaries about Neanderthal man. He was wearing a black leather jacket and faded jeans. As usual he had a couple of medallions buried in the forest of hair that sprouted up his chest and out of his open-necked shirt. Boyle looked more criminal than a criminal. He wasn't someone you'd want to meet on a dark night. He wasn't someone you'd want to meet at all.

"This is incredible!" Tim exclaimed. He turned to me. "You remember the horoscope

* See *Public Enemy Number Two*

in the newspaper! It said I was going to meet an old friend!"

"I'm not an old friend!" Snape exploded. "I hate you!"

"*I'd* like to get friendly with him," Boyle muttered. He took out a knuckleduster and slid it over his right fist. "Why don't you let the two of us go somewhere quiet, Chief...?"

"Forget it, Boyle!" Snape snapped. "And where did you get the knuckleduster? Have you been in the evidence room again?"

"It's mine!" Boyle protested.

"Well, put it away..."

Boyle slid the contraption off his hand and sulked.

Snape sat down behind his desk. Tim and I were sitting opposite him. We'd been waiting for him in the office for a couple of hours but he hadn't offered either of us so much as a cup of tea.

"What I want to know," he began, "is what the two of you were doing at the circus tonight. Why were the performers trying to kill you? And what happened to Boris the balloon-seller?"

"Someone killed him," I said.

"I know that, laddy. I've seen the body. Someone stuck a knife in him."

"Yeah." I nodded. "The circus people thought it was us."

"That's an easy enough mistake to make

when you two are involved." Snape smiled mirthlessly. "We went to the circus because we wanted to talk to the balloon-seller," he explained. "Luckily for you. But why were you interested in him? That's what I want to know."

"I wanted to buy a balloon," I said.

"Don't lie to me, Diamond! Not unless you want to spend a few minutes on your own with Boyle."

"Just one minute," Boyle pleaded. "Thirty seconds!"

"All right," I said. "We were interested in Lenny Smile."

"Ah!" Snape's eyes widened. Boyle looked disappointed. "Why?"

"We're working for a man called Joe Carter. He's American…"

"He thinks Lenny Smile was murdered," Tim said.

Snape nodded. "Of course Smile was murdered," he said. "And it was the best thing that ever happened to him. If I wasn't a police-man, I'd have been tempted to murder him myself."

Tim stared. "But he was a saint!" he burbled.

"He was a crook! Lenny Smile was the biggest crook in London! Boyle and I have been investigating him for months – and we'd have arrested him if he hadn't gone under that steamroller." Snape opened a drawer and took out a file as thick as a north London telephone directory. "This is the file on Lenny Smile," he said. "Where do you want me to begin?"

"How about at the beginning?" I suggested.

"All right. Lenny Smile set up a charity called Dream Time. He employed two assistants ... Rodney Hoover, who comes from the Ukraine. And Fiona Lee. She's from Sloane Square. We've investigated them, and as far as we can see they're in the clear. But Smile? He was a different matter. All the money passed through his bank account. He was in financial control. And half the money that went in, never came out."

"You mean ... he stole it?" I asked.

"Exactly. Millions of pounds that should have gone to poor children went into his own pocket. And when he did spend money on children, he got everything cheap. He provided hospitals with cheap X-ray machines that could only see halfway through. He provided schools with cheap books full of typing errrors. He took a bunch of children on a cheap adventure holiday."

"What's wrong with that?"

"It was in Afghanistan! Half the children still haven't come back! He bought headache pills that actually gave you a headache and food parcels where the parcels tasted better than the food. I'm telling you, Diamond, Lenny Smile was so crooked he makes an evening with Jack the Ripper sound like a nice idea! And I was this close to arresting him." Snape held his thumb and forefinger just millimetres apart. "I already had a full-time police officer watching his flat. It's like I say. We were just going to arrest him – but then he got killed."

"Suppose he isn't dead," I said.

Snape shook his head. "There were too many witnesses. Mrs Lovely, the woman who lived next door, saw him leave the flat. Hoover and Lee were with him. There was Barry Krishner, the driver. And Boris..."

"Wait a minute!" I interrupted. "Mrs Lovely didn't actually see anything. Barry Krishner has gone mad. I'm not sure Hoover and Lee can be trusted. And someone has just killed Boris." I remembered what Mrs Lovely had told us. "Mrs Lovely said that someone had been asking questions about the balloon-seller," I went on. "I thought she was talking about you ... the police! But now I wonder if it wasn't someone else. The real killer, for example!" Snape stared at me. "I think Boris saw what really happened," I concluded. "And that was why he was killed."

"Who by?" Snape demanded.

"By Lenny Smile!"

There was a long silence. Snape looked doubtful. Boyle looked ... well the same way Boyle always looks.

"What do you mean?" Snape demanded at length.

"It all makes sense. Lenny Smile knew that you were after him. You say you had a policeman watching his flat?"

Snape nodded. "Henderson. He's disappeared."

"Since when?"

"He vanished a week before the accident with the steamroller..."

"That was no accident!" I said. "Don't you get it, Snape? Smile knew he was cornered. You were closing in on him. And Joe Carter was coming over too. Carter wanted to know what had happened to all the millions he'd given Dream Time. So Smile had to disappear. He faked his own death, and right now he's somewhere in London. We've seen him! Twice!"

That made Snape sit up. "Where?"

"He was at the circus. He was in the crowd. We saw him about a minute before Boris was killed. And he was at the cemetery. Not underground – on top of it! I followed him and he ran away."

"How do you know it was Smile?" Snape asked.

"I don't. At least, I can't be sure. But I've seen a photograph of him and it looked the same."

"We don't know much about Smile," Snape

71

admitted. "Henderson was watching the flat, but he only saw him once. We know when he was born and when he died. But that's about all..."

"He didn't die. I'm telling you. Dig up the coffin and you'll probably find it's empty!"

Snape looked at Boyle, then back at me. Slowly, he nodded. "All right, laddy," he said. "Let's play it your way. But if you're wasting my time ... it's your funeral!"

"There was no funeral," I said. "Lenny Smile isn't dead."

"Let's find out..."

I'll tell you now. There's one place you don't want to be at five past twelve on a black November night – and that's in a cemetery. The ground was so cold I could feel it all the way up to my knees, and every time I breathed the ice seemed to find its way into my skull. There were the four of us there – Snape, Boyle, Tim and myself – and now we'd been joined by another half-dozen police officers and workmen, two of whom were operating a mechanical digger that whined and groaned as it clawed at the frozen earth. Tim was whining and groaning too, as a matter of fact. I think he'd have preferred to have been in bed.

But maybe it wasn't just the weather that was managing to chill me. The whole thing was like a scene out of *Frankenstein*. You know the one – where Igor the deformed Hungarian servant has to climb into the grave and steal a human brain. Glancing at Boyle, I saw a distinct physical resemblance. I had to remind myself that two days ago I had been enjoying half-term and that the following day I would be back at school, with all the fun of double geography and French. In the meantime I had somehow stumbled into a horror film. I wondered what was going to turn up in the final reel.

The digger stabbed down. The earth shifted. Gradually the hole got deeper. There was a clunk – metal hitting wood – and two of the workmen climbed in to clear away the rest of the soil with spades. Snape moved forward.

I didn't watch as the coffin was opened. You have to remember that I was only fourteen years old, and if someone had made a film out of what was going on here I wouldn't even have been allowed to see it.

"Boyle!" Snape muttered the single word and the other man lowered himself into the hole. There was a pause. Then…

"Sir!"

Boyle was holding something. He passed it up to Snape. It was dark blue, shaped a bit like a bell, only paper thin. There was a silver disc squashed in the middle. It took me a few seconds to work out what it was. Then I realized. It was a police-constable's helmet.

But one that had been flattened.

"Henderson!" Snape muttered.

There had been a police-constable watching Smile's flat. He had disappeared a week before the accident. His name had been Henderson.

And now we knew what had happened to him.

"Don't you see, Tim? It was Henderson who was killed. Not Lenny Smile!"

The two of us were back at our Camden flat. After our hours spent in the cemetery, we were too cold to go to bed. I'd made us both hot chocolate and Tim was wearing two pairs of pyjamas and two dressing-gowns, with a hot-water bottle clasped to his chest.

"But who killed him?"

"Lenny Smile."

"But what about Hoover? And the woman? They were there when it happened."

For once, Tim was right. Rodney Hoover and Fiona Lee must have been part of it. Snape had already gone to arrest them. The man they had helped down the stairs must have been Henderson. I had been right about that. He had been drugged. They had taken him out of the flat and thrown him into the road, just as Barry Krishner turned the corner on his way home...

And yet it wasn't going to be easy to prove. There were no witnesses. And until Smile was found, it was hard to see exactly what he could do. Suddenly I realized how clever Smile had been. The blurred man? He had been more than that. He had run Dream Time, he had stolen all the money, and he had remained virtually invisible.

"Nobody knew him." I said.

"Who?"

"Smile. Mrs Lovely never spoke to him. Joe Carter only wrote to him. We went to his flat and it was like he'd never actually lived there. Even Rodney Hoover and Fiona Lee couldn't tell us much about him."

Tim nodded. I yawned. It was two o'clock, way past my bedtime. And in just five and a half hours I'd be getting ready for school. Monday was going to be a long day.

"You'll have to go to the Ritz tomorrow," I said.

"Why?"

"To tell Joe Carter about his so-called best friend."

Tim sighed. "It's not going to be easy," he said. "He had this big idea about Lenny Smile when all the time he was someone else!"

I finished my hot chocolate and stood up. Then, suddenly, it hit me. "What did you just say?" I asked.

"I've forgotten." Tim was so tired he was forgetting what he was saying even as he said it.

"Someone else! That's exactly the point! Of course!"

There had been so many clues. The note in the cemetery. Mrs Lovely and the card Lenny had sent her. The gravestone. The photograph of Smile outside the Café Debussy. And Snape...

"We know when he was born..."

But it was only now, when I was almost too tired to move, that it came together. The truth. All of it.

The following morning, I didn't go to school. Instead I made two telephone calls, and then later on, just after ten o'clock, Tim and I set out for the final showdown.

It was time to meet Lenny Smile.

THE BIG WHEEL

The tube from Camden Town to Waterloo is direct on the Northern line – which was probably just as well. I'd only had about five hours' sleep, and I was so tired that the whole world seemed to be shimmering and moving in slow motion. Tim was just as bad. He had a terrible nightmare in which he was lowered, still standing up, into Lenny's grave – and woke up screaming. I suppose it wasn't too surprising. He'd fallen asleep on the escalator.

But the two of us had livened up a little by the time we'd reached the other end. The weather had taken a turn for the worse. The rain was sheeting down, sucking any colour or warmth out of the city. We had left Waterloo station behind us, making for the South Bank, a stretch of London that has trouble looking beautiful even on the sunniest day. This is where you'll find the National Theatre and the National Film Theatre, both designed by architects with huge buckets of prefabricated cement. There weren't many people around. Just a few commuters struggling with umbrellas that the wind had turned inside out. Tim and I hurried forward without speaking. The rain lashed down, hit the concrete and bounced up again, wetting us twice.

I had made the telephone call just after breakfast.

"*Mrs Lee?*"

"*Yes. Who is this?*" Fiona Lee's clipped vowels had been instantly recognizable down the line.

"*This is Nick Diamond. Remember me?*"

A pause.

"*I want to meet with Lenny Smile.*"

A longer pause. Then, "*That's not possible. Lenny Smile is dead.*"

"*You're lying. You know where he is. I want to see the three of you. Hoover, Lenny and you. Eleven o'clock at the London Eye. And if you don't want me to go to the police, you'd better not be late.*"

You've probably seen the London Eye, the huge Ferris wheel they put up outside County Hall. It's one of the big surprises of modern London. Unlike the Millennium Dome, it has actually been a success. It opened on time. It worked. It didn't fall over. At the end of the millennium year they decided to keep it, and suddenly it was part of London – a brilliant silver circle at once huge and yet somehow fragile. Tim had taken me on it for my fourteenth birthday and we'd enjoyed the view so much we'd gone a second time. Well as they say, one good turn deserves another.

Not that we were going to see much today. The clouds were so low that the pods at the top almost seemed to disappear into them. You could see the Houses of Parliament on the other side of the river and, hazy in the distance, St Paul's. But that was about it. If there was a single day in the year when it wasn't worth paying ten pounds for the ride, this was it, which would explain why there were no crowds around when we approached: just Rodney Hoover and Fiona Lee, both of them wearing raincoats, waiting for us to arrive.

There was no sign of Lenny Smile, but I wasn't surprised. I had known he would never show up.

"Why are you calling us?" Hoover demanded. "First we have the police accusing us of terrible things. Then you, wanting to see Lenny. We don't know where Lenny is! As far as we know, he's dead..."

"Why don't we get out of the rain?" I suggested. "How about the wheel?" It seemed like a good idea. The rain was still bucketing down and there was nowhere else to go.

"After you, Mr Hoover..."

We bought tickets and climbed into the first compartment that came round. I wasn't surprised to find that there would only be the four of us in it for this turn of the wheel. The doors slid shut, and slowly – so slowly that we barely knew we were moving – we were carried up into the sky, into the driving rain.

There was a pause as if nobody knew quite what to say. Then Fiona broke the silence. "We already told that ghastly little policeman ... Detective Chief Inspector Snape. Lenny was with us that day. He was killed by the steam-roller. And it is Lenny buried in the cemetery."

"No it isn't," I said. "Lenny Smile is right here now. He's on the big wheel. Inside this compartment."

"Is he?" Tim looked under the seat. "I don't see him!"

"That's because you're not looking in the right place, Tim," I said. "But that was the whole idea. You said it yourself last night. We all thought Lenny Smile was one thing, but in fact he was something else."

"You are not making the lot of sense," Hoover said. His face, already dark to begin with, had gone darker. He was watching me with nervous eyes.

"I should have known from the start that there was something strange about Lenny Smile," I said. "Nothing about him added up. Nobody – except you – had ever seen him. And

80

everything about him was a lie."

"You mean ... his name wasn't Lenny Smile?" Tim asked.

"Lenny Smile never existed, Tim!" I explained. "He was a fantasy. I should have known when I saw the details on the gravestone. It said that he was born on 31st April 1955. But that was the first lie. There are only thirty days in April. 31st April doesn't exist!"

"It was a mistake..." Fiona muttered.

"Maybe. But then there was that photograph Carter showed us of 'Lenny' standing outside the Café Debussy. You told us that he was allergic to a lot of things, and one of those things was animals. But in the photograph there's a cat sitting between his feet – and he doesn't seem to care. The allergy business was a lie. But it was a clever one. It meant that he had a reason not to be seen. He had to stay indoors because he was ill..."

Centimetre by centimetre, the big wheel carried us further away from the ground. The rain was hammering against the glass. Looking out, I could barely see the buildings on the north bank of the river. There was Big Ben, but then the rain swept across it, turning it into a series of brown and white streaks.

Tim gaped. "So there was no Lenny Smile!" he exclaimed.

"That's right. Except when Hoover *pretended* to be Lenny Smile. Don't you see? He rented the flat even though he never actually lived there. Occasionally he went in and out to make it look as if there was someone there. And of course it was Hoover who wrote that letter to Mrs Lovely."

"How do you know?"

"Because it was written in green ink. The message we saw in the card on Lenny's grave was also written in green ink – and it was the same handwriting. I should have seen from the start. It was Hoover we saw at the circus. And he was also there at Brompton Cemetery the day we visited the grave. I should have known it was him as soon as we met him at the Dream Time office."

"Why?" Tim asked.

"Because Hoover had never met us – but somehow he knew we'd been to Brompton Cemetery. Don't you remember what he said to us? 'You know very well that he's lying there in Brompton Cemetery.' Those were his exact words. But he only knew we knew because he knew who we were, and he knew who we were because he'd seen us!"

Tim scratched his head. "Could you say that last bit again?"

Fiona looked at me scornfully. "You're talking tommy-rot!" she said.

"Was Tommy part of this too?" Tim asked.

"Why would Rodney and I want to invent a man called Lenny Smile?" she continued, ignoring him.

"Because the two of you were stealing millions of pounds from Dream Time. You knew that eventually the police would catch up with you. And there was always the danger that someone like Joe Carter would come over from America to find out what was happening to his money. You were the brains behind the charity. You were the 'big wheels', if you like. But you needed someone to take the blame and then disappear. That was Lenny Smile. Henderson – the policeman – must have found out what was going on, so he had to die too. And that was your brilliant idea. You'd turn Henderson into Lenny Smile. He went under the steam-roller and, as far as you were concerned, that was the end of the matter. Smile was dead. There was nothing left to investigate."

The pod was still moving up. There were a few pedestrians out on the South Bank. By now they were no more than dots.

"But now the police think Lenny Smile is alive," I went on. "That's why the two of you aren't in jail. They're looking for him. They don't have any proof against you. So the two of you are in the clear!"

Hoover had listened to all this in silence but now he smiled, his thin lips peeling back from his teeth. "You have it exactly right," he said. "Fiona and I are nobodies. We were just working for Lenny Smile. He is the real crook.

And, as you say, they have no proof. Nobody has any proof."

"Hoover dressed up as Lenny Smile…" Tim was still trying to work it all out.

"Only once. For the photograph that Joe Carter requested. But he was wearing the same coat and the same gloves when we saw him – which is why we thought he was Lenny Smile. Both times, he was too far away for us to see his face. And, of course, in the photograph the face was purposely blurred." I turned to Rodney. "I'd be interested to know, though. What were you doing in the cemetery?"

Hoover shrugged. "I realized that the bloody fool of an undertaker had made a mistake with the date on the gravestone. I went there to put it right. When I saw you and your brother at the grave, I knew something was wrong. I have to admit, I panicked. And ran."

"And the circus…?"

"Mrs Lovely told us there had been a witness. I had to track him down and make sure he didn't talk."

"But it wouldn't have mattered if he'd talked," Tim said. "He was Russian! Nobody would have understood."

"I don't believe in taking chances," Rodney said. His hand had slid into his coat pocket. Why wasn't I surprised, when it came out, to see that it was holding a gun?

"He's got a gun!" Tim squealed.

"That's right, Tim," I said.

"You've been very clever," Hoover snarled. "But you haven't quite thought it through." He glanced out of the window. We had reached the top of the circle, as high up as the Ferris wheel went. Suddenly Hoover fired. The glass door smashed. Tim leapt. The rain came rushing in. "An unfortunate accident!" Hoover shouted above the howl of the wind. "The door malfunctioned. Somehow it broke. You and your brother fell out."

"No we didn't!" Tim whimpered.

"Anyway, by the time they've finished wiping you off the South Bank, Fiona and I will have disappeared. The money is in a nice little bank in Brazil. We'll move there. A beach house in Rio de Janeiro! We'll live a life of luxury."

"That money was meant for sick children!" I shouted. "Don't you have any shame at all?"

"I cannot afford shame!" He gestured with the gun, pointing at the shattered glass and the swirling rain. "Now which one of you is going to step out first?"

"He is!" Tim pointed at me.

"No, I'm not," I said. I turned back to Hoover. "It won't work, Hoover. Why don't you take a look in the next pod?"

Hoover's eyes narrowed. Fiona Lee went over to the window. There were about twenty people in the pod above us on the London Eye.

All of them were dressed in blue. "It's full of policemen!" she exclaimed. She went over to the other side. "And the one below us! That's full of police too!"

"It must be their day out!" Tim said.

"Forget it, Tim." It was my turn to smile. "You've been set up, Hoover. Every word you've said has been recorded. The pod's bugged. Your confession is on tape right now, and as soon as the ride is over you and Fiona will have another ride. To jail!"

Fiona had begun to tremble. Hoover's eyes twitched. His grip tightened on the gun. "Maybe I'll kill you anyway," he said. "Just for the fun of it…"

And that was when the helicopter appeared – a dark-blue police helicopter, its blades beating at the rain outside the broken window. It had come swooping out of the clouds and now hovered just a few metres away. I could see Snape in the passenger seat. Boyle was in the back, dressed in a flak jacket, cradling an automatic rifle. I just hoped he was pointing it at Hoover, not at Tim.

"Why do you think the police released you?" I shouted above the noise of the helicopter. "I rang Snape this morning and told him what I'd worked out and he asked me to meet you. You walked into a trap. He knew you'd feel safe up in the air, just the four of us. He wanted you to confess."

A second later there was a crackle and Snape's voice came, amplified, from the helicopter. "Put the gun down, Hoover! The pod is surrounded!"

Hoover swore in Ukrainian, and before I could stop him he had twisted round and fired at the helicopter.

I threw myself at Hoover.

He fired a second time. But his aim had gone wild. The bullet hit Fiona in the shoulder. She screamed and fell to her knees.

Hoover, with my hands at his throat, crashed into the window. This one didn't break. I heard the toughened glass clunk against his un-toughened skull. His eyes glazed and he slid to the ground.

I turned to Tim. "Are you all right, Tim?" I asked.

"Yes, I'm fine." He pointed past the helicopter. "Look! You can see Trafalgar Square!"

It took another fifteen minutes for the pod to reach the ground. At once we were surrounded by uniformed police officers. Hoover and Lee were dragged out. They'd spend a few days in hospital on their way to jail. The helicopter with Snape and Boyle in was nowhere to be seen. With a bit of luck a strong gust of wind would have blown it out of London and maybe into Essex. The trouble with those two was that no matter how many times we helped them, they'd never thank us.

And I'd probably end up with a detention for missing a day of school.

"We'd better go to the Ritz," I said.

"For tea?" Tim asked.

"No, Tim. Joe Carter..."

The American was still waiting to hear about his best friend, Lenny Smile. I wasn't looking forward to breaking the bad news to him. Maybe I'd leave that to Tim. After all, discreet was his middle name.

It had stopped raining. Tim and I walked along the South Bank, leaving the London Eye behind us. There were workmen ahead of us, shovelling a rich, black ooze onto the surface of the road. On the pavement, a tramp stood with an upturned hat, playing some sort of plinky-plonk music on a strange instrument – a zither, I think. I found a pound coin and dropped it into the hat. Charity. That was how this had all begun.

"Ta!" the tramp said.

"Tar? Don't worry," Tim said. "I've seen it..."

We crossed the river, the sound of the zither fading into the distance behind.

I KNOW WHAT YOU DID LAST WEDNESDAY

AN INVITATION

I like horror stories – but not when they happen to me. If you've read my other adventures, you'll know that I've been smothered in concrete, thrown in jail with a dangerous lunatic, tied to a railway line, almost blown up, chased through a cornfield dodging machine-gun bullets, poisoned in Paris ... and all this before my fourteenth birthday. It's not fair. I do my homework. I clean my teeth twice a day. Why does everyone want to kill me?

But the worst thing that ever happened to me began on a hot morning in July. It was the first week of the summer holidays and there I was, as usual, stuck with my big brother Tim, the world's most unsuccessful private detective. Tim had just spent a month helping with security at the American Embassy in Grosvenor Square and even now I'm not sure how he'd decided that there was a bomb in the ambassador's car. Anyway, just as the ambassador was about to get in, Tim had grabbed hold of him and hurled him out of the way – which would have been heroic if there had been a bomb (there wasn't) and if Tim hadn't managed to throw the unfortunate man in front of a passing bus. The ambassador was now in hospital. And Tim was out of work.

So there we were at the breakfast table with Tim reading the morning post while I counted out the cornflakes. We were down to our last packet and it had to last us another week. That allowed us seventeen flakes each but as a treat I'd allowed Tim to keep the free toy. There was a handful of letters that morning and so far they'd all been bills.

"There's a letter from Mum," Tim said.

"Any money?"

"No…"

He quickly read the letter. It was strange to think that my mum and dad were still in Australia and that I would have been with them if I hadn't slipped off the plane and gone to stay with Tim. My dad was a door-to-door salesman, selling doors. He had a house in Sydney with three bedrooms and forty-seven doors. It had been two years now since I had seen him.

"Mum says you're welcome to visit," Tim said. "She says the door is always open."

"Which one?" I asked.

He picked up the last letter. I could see at

once that this wasn't a bill. It came in a square, white envelope made out of the sort of paper that only comes from the most expensive trees. The address was handwritten: a fountain-pen, not a biro. Tim weighed it in his hand. "I wonder what this is," he said.

"It's an envelope, Tim," I replied. "It's what letters come in."

"I mean … I wonder who it's from!" He smiled. "Maybe it's a thank-you letter from the American ambassador."

"Why should he thank you? You threw him under a bus!"

"Yes, but I sent him a bunch of grapes in hospital."

"Just open it, Tim," I said.

Tim grabbed hold of a knife, and – with a dramatic gesture – sliced open the mysterious envelope.

After we'd finished bandaging his left leg, we examined the contents. First, there was an invitation, printed in red ink on thick white card.

Dear Herbert, it began. Tim Diamond was, of course, only the name he called himself. His real name was Herbert Simple.

It has been many years since we met, but I would like to invite you to a reunion of old boys and girls from St Egbert's Comprehensive, which will take place from Wednesday 9th to Friday 11th July. I am sure you are busy

*but I am so keen to see you again that I will
pay you £1,000 to make the journey to Scotland. I also enclose a ticket for the train.
Your old friend,
Rory McDougal*

Crocodile Island, Scotland

Tim tilted the envelope. Sure enough, a first-
class train ticket slid out onto the table.

"That's fantastic!" Tim exclaimed. "A first-
class ticket to Scotland." He examined the
ticket. "And back again! That's even better!"

"Wait a minute," I said. "Who is Rory
McDougal?" But even as I spoke, I thought
the name was familiar.

"We were at school together, in the same
class. Rory was brilliant. He came first in
maths. He was so clever, he passed all his
exams without even reading the questions.
After he left school, he invented the pocket
calculator – which was just as well, because
he made so much money he needed a pocket
calculator to count it."

"McDougal Industries." Now I knew where
I'd heard the name. McDougal had been in the
newspapers. The man was a multi-Mcmillion-
aire.

"When did you last see him?" I asked.

"It must have been on prize-giving day,
about ten years ago," Tim said. "He went to

university, I joined the police."

Tim had only spent a year with the police but in that time the crime rate had doubled. He didn't often talk about it but I knew that he had once put together an identikit picture that had led to the arrest of the Archbishop of Canterbury. He'd been transferred to the mounted police but that had only lasted a few weeks before his horse resigned. Then he'd become a private detective – and of course, *he* had hardly made millions. If you added up all the money Tim had ever made and put it in a bank, the bank wouldn't even notice.

"Are you going?" I asked.

Tim flicked a cornflake towards his mouth. It disappeared over his shoulder. "Of course I'm going," he said. "Maybe McNoodle will offer me a job. Head of Security on Alligator Island."

"Crocodile Island, Tim." I picked up the invitation. "What about me?"

"Sorry, kid. I didn't see your name on the envelope."

"Maybe it's under the stamp." Tim said nothing, so I went on, "You can't leave me here."

"Why not?"

"I'm only fourteen. It's against the law."

Tim frowned. "I won't tell if you won't tell."

"I will tell."

"Forget it, Nick. McStrudel is my old

schoolfriend. He went to my old school. It's my name on the envelope and you can argue all you like. But this time, I'm going alone."

We left King's Cross station on the morning of the 9th.

Tim sat next to the window, looking sulky. I was sitting opposite him. I had finally persuaded him to swap the first-class ticket for two second-class ones, which at least allowed me to travel free. You may think it strange that I should have wanted to join Tim on a journey heading several hundred miles north. But there was something about the invitation that bothered me. Maybe it was the letter, written in ink the colour of blood. Maybe it was the name – Crocodile Island. And then there was the money. The invitation might have sounded innocent enough, but why was McDougal paying Tim £1,000 to get on the train? I had a feeling that there might be more to this than a school reunion. And for that matter, why would anyone in their right mind want to be reunited with Tim?

I was also curious. It's not every day that you get to meet a man like Rory McDougal. Computers, camcorders, mobile phones and DVD players ... they all came stamped with the initials RM. And every machine that sold made McDougal a little richer.

Apparently the man was something of a

recluse. A few years back he'd bought himself an island off the Scottish coast, somewhere to be alone. There had been pictures of it in all the newspapers. The island was long and narrow with two arms jutting out and a twisting tail. Apparently, that was how it had got its name.

Tim didn't say much on the journey. To cheer him up, I'd bought him a *Beano* comic and perhaps he was having trouble with the long words. It took us about four hours to get to Scotland and it took another hour before I noticed. There were no signs, no frontier post, no man in a kilt playing the bagpipes and munching haggis as the train went past. It was only when the ticket collector asked us for our tickets and Tim couldn't understand a word he was saying that I knew we must be close. Sure enough, a few minutes later the train slowed down and Tim got out. Personally, I would have waited until the train had actually stopped, but I suppose he was over-excited.

Fortunately he was only bruised and we managed the short walk down to the harbour where an old fishing boat was waiting for us. The boat was called the *Silver Medal* and a small crowd of people were waiting to go on board.

"My God!" one of them exclaimed. "It's Herbert Simple! I never thought I'd see *him* again!"

The man who had spoken was fat and bald, dressed in a three-piece suit. If he ate much more, it would soon be a four-piece suit. His trousers were already showing the strain. His name, it turned out, was Eric Draper. He was a lawyer.

Tim smiled. "I changed my name," he announced. "It's Tim Diamond now."

They all had a good laugh at that.

"And who is he?" Eric asked. I suddenly realized he was looking at me.

"That's my kid brother, Nick."

"So what are you doing now ... Tim?" one of the women asked in a high-pitched voice. She had glasses and long, curly hair and such large teeth that she seemed to have trouble closing her mouth. Her name was Janet Rhodes.

Tim put on his "don't mess with me" face. Unfortunately, it just made him look seasick. "Actually," he drawled, "I'm a private detective."

"Really?" Eric roared with laughter. His suit shuddered and one of the buttons flew off. "I can't believe Rory invited you here too. As I recall, you were the stupidest boy at St Egbert's. I still remember your performance as Hamlet in the school play."

"What was so stupid about that?" I asked.

"Nothing. Except everyone else was doing Macbeth."

One of the other women stepped forward.

She was small and drab-looking, dressed in a mousy coat that had seen better days. She was eating a chocolate flake. "Hello ... Tim!" she said shyly. "I bet you don't remember me!"

"Of course I remember you!" Tim exclaimed. "You're Lisa Beach!"

"No I'm not! I'm Sylvie Binns." She looked disappointed. "You gave me my first kiss behind the bike shed. Don't you remember?"

Tim frowned. "I remember the bike shed..." he said.

There was a loud blast from the boat and the captain appeared, looking over the side. He had one leg, one eye and a huge beard. All that was missing was the parrot and he could have got a job in any pantomime in town. "All aboard!" he shouted. "Departing for Crocodile Island!"

We made our way up the gangplank. The boat was old and smelly. So was the captain. The eight of us stood on the deck while he pulled up the anchor, and a few minutes later we were off, the engine rattling as if it was about to fall out of the boat. It occurred to me that the Silver Medal was a strange choice of boat for a multi-millionaire. What had happened to the deluxe yacht? But nobody else had noticed, so I said nothing.

Apart from Eric, Janet and Sylvie, there were three other people on board: two more women and another man, a fit-looking black

101

guy dressed in jeans and a sweatshirt.

"That's Mark Tyler," Tim told me as we cut through the waves, leaving the mainland behind us. "He came first at sport at St Egbert's…"

I knew the name. Tyler had been in the British Olympic athletics team at Atlanta.

"He used to run to school and run home again," Tim went on. "He was so fast, he used to overtake the school bus. When he went cross-country running, he actually left the country, which certainly made the headmaster very cross. He's a brilliant sportsman!"

That just left the two other women.

Brenda Blake was an opera singer and looked it. Big and muscular, she had the sort of arms you'd expect to find on a Japanese wrestler – or perhaps around his belly.

Libby Goldman was big and blonde and worked in children's TV, presenting a television programme called *Libby's Lounge*. She sang, danced, juggled and did magic tricks … and all this before we'd even left the quay. It was a shame that in real life we couldn't turn her off.

The journey took about an hour, by which time the coast of Scotland had become just a grey smudge behind us. Slowly Crocodile Island sneaked up on us. It was about half a mile long, rising to a point at what must have been its "tail", with sheer cliffs sweeping down into the sea. There were six jagged pillars of rock at this end, making a landing impossible. But at the other end, in the shelter of the crocodile's arm, someone had built a jetty. As the boat drew in, I noticed a security camera watching us from above.

"Here we are, ladies and gentlemen," the captain announced from somewhere behind his beard. "I wish you all a very pleasant stay on Crocodile Island. I do indeed! I'll be coming back for you in a couple of days. My name is Captain Randle, by the way. Horatio Randle. It's been a pleasure having you lovely people on my boat. You remember me, now!"

"Aren't you coming with us?" Eric demanded.

"No, sir. I'm not invited," Captain Randle replied. "I live on the mainland. But I'll be back to collect you in a couple of days. I'll see you then!"

We disembarked. The boat pulled out and headed back the way it had come. The eight of us were left on the island, wondering what was going to happen next.

"So where's old Rory?" Brenda asked.

"Maybe we should walk up to the house," Sylvie suggested. She was the only one of them who didn't have a full-time job. She had told Tim that she was a housewife, and was carrying three photographs of her husband and three more of her house.

"Bit of a cheek," Eric muttered. From the look of him, walking wasn't something he did often.

"Best foot forward!" Janet said cheerily. Apparently she worked as a hairdresser, and her own hair was dancing in the wind. As indeed was Libby.

We walked. Sylvie might have called it a house but I would have said it was a castle that Rory had bought for himself on his island retreat. It was built out of grey brick: a grand, sprawling building with towers and battlements and even gargoyles gazing wickedly out of the corners. We reached the front door. It was solid oak, as thick as a tree and half as welcoming.

"I wonder if we should knock?" Tim asked.

"To hell with that!" Eric pushed and the door swung open.

We found ourselves in a great hall with a black and white floor, animal heads on the walls and a roaring fire in the hearth. A grandfather clock chimed four times. I looked at my watch – it was actually ten past three. I was already beginning to feel uneasy. Apart from the crackle of the logs and the ticking of the clock, the house was silent. It felt empty. No Rory, no Mrs Rory, no butler, no cook. Just us.

"Hello?" Libby called out. "Is there anyone at home?"

"It-doesn't-look-as-if-there's-anyone-here,"

Mark said. At least, I think that's what he said. Speaking was something else that he did very fast. Whole sentences came out of his mouth as a single word.

"This is ridiculous," Eric snapped. "I suggest we split up and try and find Rory. Maybe he's asleep upstairs."

So we all went our separate ways. Mark and Eric headed off through different doors. Libby Goldman went into the kitchen. Tim and I went upstairs. It was only now that we were inside it that I realized just how big this house was. It had five staircases, doors everywhere and so many corridors that we could have been walking through a maze. And if it looked like a castle from the outside, inside it was like a museum. There was more furniture than you'd find in a department store. Antique chairs and sofas stood next to cupboards and sideboards and tables of every shape and size. There were so many oil paintings that you could hardly see the walls. Rory also seemed to have a fondness for ancient weapons – I had only been in the place a few minutes but already I had seen crossbows and muskets and flintlock pistols mounted on wooden plaques. On the first floor there was a stuffed bear holding an Elizabethan gun … a blunderbuss. The stairs and upper landing were covered in thick, red carpet which muffled every sound. In the distance I could hear Janet calling out Rory's name but it was difficult to say if she was near or far away. Suddenly we were lost and very much on our own.

We reached a corner where there was a suit of dull silver armour standing guard; a knight with a shield but no sword.

"I don't like it," I said.

"I think it's a very nice suit of armour," Tim replied.

"I'm not talking about the armour, Tim," I said. "I'm talking about the whole island. Why isn't there anyone here to meet us? And why did your friend send that old fishing boat to pick us up?"

Tim smiled. "Relax, kid," he said. "The house is a bit quiet, that's all. But my sixth sense would tell me if there was something wrong, and right now I'm feeling fine..."

Just then there was a high-pitched scream from another part of the second floor. It was Brenda. She screamed and screamed again.

"How lovely!" Tim exclaimed. "Brenda's singing for us! I think that's Mozart, isn't it?"

"It's not Mozart, Tim," I shouted, beginning to run towards the sound. "She's screaming for help! Come on!"

We ran down the corridor and round the corner. That was when we saw Brenda, standing in front of an open bedroom door. She had stopped screaming now but her face was white and her hands were tearing at her hair. At the same time, Libby and Sylvie appeared, coming up the stairs. And Eric was also there, pushing his way forward to see what the fuss was about.

Tim and I reached the doorway. I looked inside.

The room had a red carpet. It took me a couple of seconds to realize that the room had once had a yellow carpet. It was covered in blood. There was more blood on the walls and on the bed. There was even blood on the blood.

And there was McDougal. I'm afraid it was the end of the story for Rory. The sword that had killed him was lying next to him and I guess it must have been taken from the suit of armour.

Brenda screamed again and pulled out a handful of her own hair.

Eric stood back, gasping.

Libby burst into tears.

And Tim, of course, fainted.

There were just the eight of us, trapped on Crocodile Island. And I had to admit, our reunion hadn't got off to a very good start.

AFTER DARK

"It was horrible," Tim groaned. "It was horrible. Rory McPoodle ... he was in pieces!"

"I don't want to hear about it, Tim," I said. Actually, it was too late. He'd already told me twenty times.

"Why would anyone *do* that?" he demanded. "What sort of person would do that?"

"I'm not sure," I muttered. "How about a dangerous lunatic?"

Tim nodded. "You could be right," he said.

We were sitting in our bedroom. We knew it was the bedroom that McDougal had prepared for us because it had Tim's name on the door. There were seven bedrooms on the same floor, each one of them labelled for the arriving guests. This room was square, with a high ceiling and a window with a low balcony looking out over a sea that was already grey and choppy as the sun set and the evening drew in.

There was a four-poster bed, a heavy tapestry and the sort of wallpaper that could give you bad dreams. There was also something else I'd noticed and it worried me.

"Look at this, Tim," I said. I pointed at the bedside table. "There's a telephone socket here – but no telephone. What does that tell you?"

"The last person who slept in this room stole the telephone?"

"Not exactly. I think the telephone has been taken to stop us making any calls."

"Why would anyone do that?"

"To stop us reporting the death of Rory McDougal to the police."

Tim considered. "You mean ... someone knew we were coming..." he began.

"Exactly. And they also knew we'd be stuck here. At least until the boat came back."

It was a nasty thought. I was beginning to have lots of nasty thoughts, and the worst one was this: someone had killed Rory McDougal, but had it happened before we arrived on the island? Or had he been killed by one of the people from the boat? As soon as we had arrived at the house, we had all split up. For at least ten minutes nobody had known where anybody else was, which meant that any one of us could have found Rory and killed him before the others arrived.

Along with Tim and myself, there were now six people on the island ... six and several halves if you counted Rory. Eric Draper, Janet Rhodes, Sylvie Binns, Mark Tyler, Brenda Blake and Libby Goldman. Tim hadn't seen any of them in ten years and knew hardly anything about them. Could one of them be a crazed killer? Could one of them have planned this whole thing?

I looked at my watch. It was ten to seven. We left the room and went back downstairs.

Eric Draper had called a meeting in the dining-room at seven o'clock. I don't know who had put him in charge but I guessed he had decided himself.

"He was head boy at school," Tim told me. "He was always telling everyone what to do. Even the teachers used to do what he said."

"What was Rory McDougal like as a boy?"

"Well ... he was young."

"That's very helpful, Tim. I mean ... was he popular?"

"Yes. Except he once had a big row with Libby Goldman. He tried to kiss her in biology class and she attacked him with a bicycle pump."

"But she wouldn't kill him just because of that, would she?"

"You should have seen where she put the bicycle pump!"

In fact Libby was alone in the dining-room when we arrived for the meeting. She was sitting in a chair at the end of a black, polished table that ran almost the full length of the room. Portraits of bearded men in different shades of tartan looked down from the walls. A chandelier hung from the ceiling.

She looked up as we came in. Her eyes were red. Either she had been crying or she had bad hay fever – and I hadn't noticed any hay on Crocodile Island. She was smoking a cigarette – or trying to. Her hands were shaking so much she had trouble getting it into her mouth.

"What are we going to do?" she wailed. "It's so horrible! I knew I shouldn't have accepted Rory's invitation!"

"Why did you?" I asked. "If you didn't like him…"

"Well … he's interesting. He's rich. I thought he might appear on my television programme – Libby's Lounge."

"I watch that!" Tim exclaimed.

"But it's a children's programme," Libby said.

Tim blushed. "Well … I mean … I've seen it. A bit of it."

"I've never heard of it," I muttered.

Libby's eyes went redder.

Then three of the others came in: Janet Rhodes, Mark Tyler and Brenda Blake.

"I've been trying to call the mainland on my mobile phone," Janet announced. "But I can't get a signal."

"I can't get a signal either," agreed Mark,

speaking as quickly as ever. He sort of shimmered in front of me and suddenly he was sitting down.

"There is no signal on this island."

"And no phone in my room," Janet said.

"No phone in any room!" The singer was looking pale and scared. Of course, she was the one who had found the body. Looking at her, I saw that it would be a few months before she sang in a concert hall. She probably wouldn't have the strength to sing in the bath.

Somewhere a clock struck seven and Eric Draper waddled into the room. "Are we all here?" he asked.

"I'm here!" Tim called out, as helpful as ever.

"I think there's one missing," I said.

Eric Draper did a quick head count. At least everyone in the room still had their heads. "Sylvie isn't here yet," he said. He scowled. You could tell he was the sort of man who expected everyone to do exactly what he said. "We'll have to wait for her."

"She was always late for everything," Janet muttered. She had slumped into a chair next to Libby. "I don't know how she managed to come first in chemistry. She was always late for class."

"I saw her in her room a few moments ago," Mark said. "She was sitting on the bed. She looked upset."

"I'm upset!" Eric said. "We're all upset!

Well, let's begin without her." He cleared his throat as if we were the jury and he was about to begin his summing up. "We are clearly in a very awkward situation here. We've been invited to this island, only to discover that our host, Rory McDougal, has been murdered. We can't call the police because it would seem that there are no telephones and none of our mobiles can get a signal. Unless we can find a boat to get back to the mainland, we're stuck here until Captain Randle – or whatever his name was – arrives to pick us up. The only good news is that there's plenty of food in the house. I've looked in the kitchen. This is a comfortable house. We should be fine here."

"Unless the killer strikes again," I said.

Everyone looked at me. "What makes you think he'll do that?" Eric demanded.

"It's a possibility," I said. "And anyway, 'he' could be a 'she'."

I noticed Libby shivered when I said that – but to be frank she'd been shivering a lot recently.

"Did Rory invite you here too?" Mark asked.

"Not exactly. He invited Tim, and Tim couldn't leave me on my own at home. So I came along for the ride."

Eric scowled for a second time. Scowling suited him. "I wouldn't have said this place was suitable for children," he said.

"Murder isn't suitable for children," I agreed. "But I'm stuck here with you and it seems to me that we've all been set up. No phones! That has to be on purpose. All the rooms were prepared for us, with our names on the doors. And now, like you say, we're stuck here. Suppose the killer is here too?"

"That's not possible," Brenda whispered. But she didn't sound like she believed herself.

"Maybe Rory wasn't murdered," Tim suggested. "Maybe it was an accident."

"You mean someone accidentally chopped him to pieces?" I asked.

Janet glanced at the door. She was looking nervous. A hairdresser having a bad hair day. "Perhaps we should go and find Sylvie," she suggested.

Nobody said anything. Then, as one, we hurried out of the room.

We went back upstairs. Sylvie's room was halfway down the corridor, two doors away from our own. It was closed. Tim knocked. There was no reply. "She could have fallen asleep," he said.

"Just open the door, Tim," I suggested.

He opened it. Sylvie's room was a similar size to ours but with more modern furniture, an abstract painting on the wall and two single beds. Her case was standing beside the wall, unopened. As my eyes travelled towards her, I noticed a twist of something silver lying in the

114

middle of the yellow carpet. But I didn't have time to mention it.

Sylvie was lying on her back, one hand flung out. When I had first seen her I had thought her small and silent. Now she was smaller and dreadfully still. I felt Mark push past me, entering the room.

"Is she...?" he began.

"Yes," Tim said. "She's asleep."

"I don't think so, Tim," I said.

Eric went over to her and took her wrist between a podgy finger and thumb. "She has no pulse," he said. He leant over her. "She's not breathing."

Tim's mouth fell open. "Do you think she's ill?" he asked.

"She's dead, Tim," I said. Two murders in one day. And it wasn't even Tim's bedtime.

Libby burst into tears. It was getting to be a habit with her. At least Brenda didn't scream again. At this close range, I'm not sure my eardrums could have taken it.

"What are we going to do?" someone asked. I wasn't sure who it was and it didn't matter anyway. Because right then I didn't have any idea.

"It might have been a heart attack," Tim said. "Maybe the shock of what happened to Rory..."

Darkness had fallen on Crocodile Island. It

had slithered across the surface of the sea and thrown itself over the house. Now and then a full moon came out from behind the clouds and for a moment the waves would ripple silver before disappearing into inky blackness. Tim and I were sitting on our four-poster bed. It looked like we were going to have to share it. Two posters each.

Maybe it had been a heart attack. Maybe she had died of fright. Maybe she'd caught a very bad case of flu. Everyone had their own ideas ... but I knew better. I remembered the twist of silver I had seen on the carpet.

"Tim, what can you tell me about Sylvie Binns?" I asked.

"Not a lot." Tim fell silent. "She was good at chemistry."

"I know that."

"She used to go out with Mark. We always thought the two of them would get married, but in the end she met someone else. Mark ran all the way round England. That was his way of forgetting her."

Mark Tyler had been the last person to see Sylvie alive. I wondered if he really had forgotten her. Or forgiven her.

"Maybe she was ill before she came to the island," Tim muttered.

"Tim, I think she was poisoned," I said.

"Poisoned?"

I remembered my first sight of Sylvie, on the

quay. She had been eating a chocolate flake. "Sylvie liked sweets and chocolate," I said.

"You're right, Nick! Yes. She loved chocolate. She could never resist it. When Mark was going out with her, he took her on a tour of a chocolate factory. She even ate the tickets." Tim frowned. "But what's that got to do with anything?"

"There was a piece of silver paper on the floor in her room. I think it was the wrapper off a sweet or a chocolate. Don't you see? Someone knew she couldn't resist chocolate – so they left one in her room. Maybe on her pillow."

"And it wasn't almond crunch," Tim muttered darkly.

"More likely cyanide surprise," I said.

We got into bed. Tim didn't want to turn off the lights, but a few minutes later, after he had dozed off, I reached for the switch and lay back in the darkness. I needed to think. Sylvie had eaten a poisoned chocolate. I was sure of it. But had she been given it or had she found it in her room? If it was already in the room, it could have been left there before we arrived. But if she had been given it, then the killer must still be on the island. He or she might even be in the house.

There was a movement at the window.

At first I thought I'd imagined it, but propping myself up in the bed, I saw it again. There was somebody there! No – that was impossible.

We were on the first floor. Then I remembered. There was a terrace running round the outside of the house, connecting all the bedrooms.

There it was again. I stared in horror. There was a face staring at me from the other side of the glass, a hideous skull with hollow eyes and grinning, tombstone teeth. The bones glowed in the moonlight. Now I'll be honest with you. I don't scare easily. But right then I was frozen. I couldn't move. I couldn't cry out. I'm almost surprised I didn't wet the bed.

The skull hovered in front of me. I couldn't see a body. It had to be draped in black. It's a mask, I told myself. Someone is trying to frighten you with a joke-shop mask. Somehow, I managed to force back the fear. I jerked up in bed and threw back the covers. Next to me, Tim woke up.

"Is it breakfast already?" he asked.

I ignored him. I was already darting towards the window. But at that moment, the moon vanished behind another cloud and the darkness fell. By the time I had found the lock and opened the window, the man – or woman, whoever it was – had gone.

"What is it, Nick?" Tim demanded.

I didn't answer. But it seemed that whoever had killed Rory McDougal and Sylvie Binns was still on the island.

Which left me wondering – who was going to be next?

SEARCH PARTY

Janet Rhodes didn't make it to breakfast.

There were just the five of us, sitting in the kitchen with five bowls of Frosties and a steaming plate of scrambled eggs that Brenda had insisted on cooking but which nobody felt like eating. Libby had another cigarette in her mouth but everyone had complained so much that she wasn't smoking it. She was sucking it. Eric was still in his dressing-gown, a thick red thing with his initials – ED – embroidered on the pocket. Mark was wearing a track suit. A security camera winked at us from one corner of the room. There were a lot of security cameras on the island. But none of us felt even slightly secure.

"What are we going to do?" Brenda asked. I got the feeling that she hadn't slept very much the night before. There were dark rings under her eyes and although she'd put on lipstick, most of it had missed her lips. "This island is haunted!" she went on.

"What do you mean?" Eric asked.

"Last night … my window … it was horrible."

"I've got quite a nice window," Tim said.

"I mean … I saw something! A human skull. It was dancing in the night air."

So she'd seen it too! I was about to chip in, but then Eric interrupted. "I don't think it's going to help, sharing our bad dreams," he said.

"I didn't dream it," Brenda insisted.

"We've got to do something!" Mark cut in. "First Rory, then Sylvie. At this rate, there won't be any of us left by lunch-time."

"I don't want any lunch," Libby muttered.

"We need to talk about this," Eric said. "We need to work something out. But there's no point starting until we're all here." He glanced at the clock. "Where the hell is Janet?"

"Maybe she's in the bath," Tim suggested.

"In the water or underneath it?" Eric growled.

The minute hand on the kitchen clock ticked forward. It was nine o'clock. Suddenly Mark stood up. "I'm going upstairs," he announced.

"You're going back to bed?" Tim asked.

"I'm going to find her."

He left the room. The rest of us followed

him, tiptoeing up the stairs and along the corridor with a sense of dread. Actually, Eric didn't exactly tiptoe. He was so fat that it must have been quite a few years since his toes *had* tips. Mark Tyler had moved quickly, taking the stairs four at a time as if they were hurdles and he was back at the Olympic games at Atlanta. He was outside the door when we arrived.

"She's overslept," Tim said to me. "She's fine. She's just overslept."

Eric knocked on her door. There was no answer. He knocked again, then turned the handle. The door opened.

The hairdresser had overslept all right, but nothing was ever going to wake her up again. She had been stabbed during the night. She was lying on her back on a four-poster bed like the one in our room, only smaller. The bed was old. The paint had peeled off the posts and there was a tear in the canopy above her. In fact the whole room looked shabby, as if it had been missed out by the decorators. Maybe I noticed all this because I didn't want to look at the body. You may think I'm crazy, but dead people upset me. And when I did finally look at her, I got a shock.

Whoever had killed her hadn't used a knife. There was something sticking out of her chest and at first I thought it was some sort of rocket. It was silver, in the shape of a sort of long pyramid, with four legs jutting out. Then, slowly, it dawned on me what I was looking at. It was a model, a souvenir of the building that I had climbed up with Tim only the year before.

It was incredible. But true. Janet Rhodes had been stabbed with a model of the Eiffel Tower.

"The Eiffel Tower!" Tim muttered. His face was the colour of sour milk. "It's an outrage. I mean, it's meant to be a tourist attraction!"

"Why the Eiffel Tower?" I asked.

"Because it's famous, Nick. People like to visit it."

"No – I don't mean, why is it a tourist attraction. I mean, why use it as a murder weapon? It's certainly a strange choice. Maybe someone is trying to tell us something."

"Well, they certainly told Janet something," Tim said.

We were back at the breakfast table. The scrambled eggs were cold and congealed and looked even less appetizing than before. All the Frosties had gone soggy. But it didn't matter. There was no way anybody was going to eat anything today. The way things were going, I wondered if any of us would ever eat anything again.

Nobody was talking very much. I knew why. But it was Brenda who put it into words.

"Do you realize..." she began, and for once

her voice was hoarse and empty. "Do you realize that the killer could be sitting here, at this table."

Tim looked around. "But there's only us here!"

"That's what she means, Tim," I said. "She's saying that the killer could be one of us!"

Brenda nodded. "I know it's one of us. One of us got up last night and went down the corridor." She shuddered. "I thought I heard squeaking last night…"

"That was Tim," I said. "He snores."

"No. It was a floorboard. Somebody left their room…"

"Did anyone else hear anything last night?" Eric asked.

There was a pause. Then Libby nodded. "I have the room next to Mark," she said. She turned to look at him. "I heard your door open just after midnight. I heard you go into the corridor."

"I went to the toilet," Mark replied. His dark face had suddenly got darker. He didn't like being accused.

"You went to the toilet in the corridor?" Tim asked.

"I went to the toilet which is across the corridor, opposite my room. I didn't go anywhere near Janet."

"What about the skull?" Brenda whispered.

Eric scowled. He had forgotten about the dancing skull. "I know you say it's a dream, Eric," she went on. "But that's typical of you. You never believed anything I said, even when we were at school. Well, believe me now..." she took a deep breath. "Maybe it wasn't a ghost or a monster. Maybe it was someone in a mask. But they were there! I was awake. I jumped out of bed and went over to the window but by the time I got there, seconds later, they'd gone. Vanished into thin air..."

"It wasn't a dream," I said. "I saw it too."

"You?" Eric sneered at me.

I nodded.

"I didn't see anything," Tim said.

"You were asleep, Tim. But it was definitely there. It came out of nowhere ... like a magic trick. A rabbit out of a hat!"

"You saw a rabbit too?" Tim asked.

We all ignored him. "Any one of us could have climbed out onto the terrace," Brenda said. "Any one of us could have killed Janet. And Rory. And Sylvie! How do we know that she wasn't strangled or poisoned or something?"

"I think she *was* poisoned," I said.

Everyone looked at me so I told them about the sweet wrapper and Sylvie's love of chocolate. It was strange. Everyone in the room was ten years older than me but suddenly I was in control.

Not for long, though. Eric Draper, the ex-head boy, raised his hands. "Ladies and gentlemen," he announced. "I don't think we should jump to conclusions. Why would any of us sitting at this table want to kill Rory or Sylvie or Janet?"

"Mark used to go out with Sylvie," Libby said. She was staring at him. "When she broke up with you, you told me you wanted to kill her."

"That was ten years ago!" Mark protested. He jerked a finger at Libby. "Anyway, what about *you*? You nearly *did* kill Rory with that bicycle pump..."

"Yes. And what about you!" Tim pointed at Eric. "You say your name's Eric, so why are you wearing a dressing-gown that belongs to Ed?"

It took Eric a few seconds to work out what Tim was getting at. "Those are my initials, you idiot!" he snapped. He took a deep breath and raised his hands. "Look," he went on. "There's no point arguing amongst ourselves. We have to stick together. It could be our only hope."

The others fell silent. I had to admit, Eric was speaking sense. Blaming each other wouldn't help.

"Both Brenda and ... Tim's little brother saw somebody last night," he went on. I didn't know why he couldn't call me by my name.

"Now that could have been one of us, dressing up to frighten the others. But remember, we were all inside the house … and this thing, whatever it was, was outside. So maybe it was someone else. Maybe it was someone we don't know about."

"You mean … someone hiding on the island?" Mark said.

"Exactly. We know we can't call the police. We know we're stuck here. But it seems to me that the first thing we have to do is find out if there's anyone else here."

"We've got to organize a search party," I said.

Tim shook his head. "This is no time for a party, Nick," he muttered.

"You're right, Eric," Libby said. "We've got to go over the island from head to tail."

"But at the same time, I think we should keep an eye on each other," Brenda said. "I'll feel safer that way."

Eric went upstairs to get changed. Mark went with him. From now on, we were going to do everything in pairs. Brenda and Libby cleared the breakfast things. I'd already noticed that most of the food in the house was in tins – which was just as well. Even the cleverest killer couldn't tamper with a tin, so at least we wouldn't starve. At half past nine we all met in the hall. Then we put on our coats and went outside.

The search began back at the jetty, right at the head of the crocodile. The idea was that we could cover the entire island, working like the police searching a wood when someone has gone missing. That is, we kept ten metres apart, always in sight of one another, moving across the island in a line. It was a beautiful day. The sun was shining and the sea was blue, but even so I could feel a chill breeze on Crocodile Island. And there was something else. I couldn't escape the feeling that I was being watched. It was weird. Because it was obvious that there wasn't anybody in sight ... not even so much as a sheep or a cow.

It only took us an hour to cover the island. There really wasn't very much there. Most of it was covered in gorse that only came up to the knee, which no killer could have hidden behind – unless, of course, he happened to be extremely small. There were a few trees but we checked the branches and Tim even climbed one to see if anyone was hiding at the top. Then I climbed up to help Tim down again and we moved on. We came to a couple of ruined outbuildings. I went inside. There was nobody there – but I did see something. Another security camera, fixed to the brickwork. Of course, a rich man like Rory would have had to be careful about security. I remembered the camera I had noticed in the kitchen. He had probably covered the whole island. Was that why I had felt we were being watched?

We went past the house and continued towards the crocodile's tail. The ground rose steeply up, finally arriving at a narrow point at least twenty metres above the sea. This was what I had seen from the boat. Six great rocks, steel grey and needle-sharp, rose out of the water far below. Looking down made my head spin. I wondered briefly if there might be a cave somewhere, perhaps tucked underneath the lip where we were standing. But then a wave rolled in, crashing against the cliff face. If there was a killer down there, he'd be soaking wet. And anyway, as far as I could see, there was no way down.

We moved away, retracing our steps. There was nobody outside the house, but how about inside? Starting in the hall, we went from room to room: the library, the dining-room, the conservatory, the hall and so on. We looked behind curtains, under tables, in the fireplaces and up the chimneys. Tim even looked in the grandfather clocks. Maybe he thought he'd find somebody's grandfather. We covered the ground floor and then went up to the first. Here were the bedrooms, with our names still attached to the doors. We went into every one of them. There was nobody there ... apart from the three very dead bodies. It wasn't easy searching those particular rooms, but we made ourselves ... although I think Tim was wasting his time doing it with his eyes tightly shut.

Nobody in the rooms. Nobody in the corridors. We found the attic but all that was there was a water tank. Tim dipped his head in and I made a mental note not to drink any more water. Not with his dandruff. Eventually, we gave up. We had been everywhere. There was nowhere else to look.

We started to go back down to the kitchen but had only got halfway there when Libby let out a little gasp.

"What is it?" Eric demanded.

"There." She pointed at the wall at the end of the corridor. "I don't know why I didn't see it before!"

What she had seen was a black-and-white photograph in a silver frame. It was hanging right in the middle of the wall with enough space around it to make it stand out. The question was – had Rory hung it there? Or had it been someone else? Was this something we were meant to see?

The photograph showed nine teenagers, all of them wearing the same uniform. It's funny how people change in ten years – but I recognized them at once: Eric Draper, Janet Rhodes, Mark Tyler, Brenda Blake, Sylvie Binns, Libby Goldman, Rory McDougal and Tim. Tim looked the weirdest of them all. He'd had long hair then, and spots. Lots of spots. Of course, I wouldn't have looked too great myself when the picture had been taken – but then I would only have been four years old.

There was one face, however, that I didn't know. He was standing at the edge of the group, slightly apart; a thin, gangly teenager with curly hair and glasses. He was wearing an anorak and had the sort of face you'd expect to see on a train-spotter. "Who's he?" I asked.

"That's Johnny!" Brenda replied. "Johnny Nadler. He was one of my best friends…"

"And mine," Libby agreed. "Everyone liked Johnny. We used to hang out with him in the yard." She walked closer to the photograph. "I remember when this was taken. It was prize-giving day. He came second in geography. I came first."

"Wait a minute," I interrupted. "Everyone in this photograph is here on Crocodile Island. Everyone except Johnny Nadler!"

"You're right!" Mark agreed. "Why wasn't he invited?"

"Because he's the killer!" Eric snapped. "He's got to be!"

"But why would Johnny want to kill Rory?" Brenda asked. "The two of them were friends. And every day after school he used to catch the bus with Sylvie – even though it took him eight miles in the wrong direction. That's how much he liked her."

"He let Janet cut his hair," Libby went on. "She accidentally cut a chunk out of his ear, but he didn't mind. In fact he laughed all the way to the hospital. Johnny wouldn't hurt anyone."

"What else can you tell me about him?" I asked.

"He came second in history as well as geography," Eric said. "He was really clever."

"He was always playing with model planes and cars," Mark added. "He used to build them himself. We always said he'd be an inventor when he left school but in fact he ended up working at Boots. I saw him there once, when I went in to get some ointment." He blushed. "I had athlete's foot."

"Did any of the rest of you ever see him again?" I asked.

Everyone shook their heads. I looked at the photograph again. It did seem strange that he was the only one in the picture who hadn't been invited to Crocodile Island. But did that make him the killer? And if so, where on earth was he? We had searched the entire island and we were certain now that we were the only ones who were there.

Eric looked at his watch. It was half past twelve. "I suggest we continue this meeting downstairs," he said.

"I need to change," Brenda said.

"Me too," Libby agreed.

Everyone started to move in different directions.

"Hold on a minute!" I said. "I thought we were all going to stick together. I think we should all stay in this room."

"Don't be ridiculous!" Eric snapped. "We have to eat something. It's lunch-time. And anyway, we've just searched the island. We know there's nobody else here."

"Well, I'm staying with Tim," I said.

"How do you know I'm not the killer?" Tim demanded.

Because whoever killed Rory and the others is brilliant and fiendish and you still have trouble tying your shoelaces. That was what I thought, but I didn't say anything. I just shrugged.

"I don't want to be near anyone," Libby said. "I feel safer on my own."

"Me too." Brenda nodded. "And I'm certainly not having anyone in the room with me while I'm changing."

"We can meet in ten minutes," Eric said. "We're inside the house. We know there's nobody else on the island. We'll meet in the dining-room at twenty to one."

He was wrong of course. This was one little group that was never going to meet again. But how could we know that? We were scared and we weren't thinking straight.

Tim and I went back to our room. Tim scratched his head, which was still damp from the water tank. "Johnny could be hiding on

132

the island," he said. "What if there's a secret room?"

The same thought had already occurred to me, but I'd tapped every wall and every wooden panel and nothing had sounded hollow. "I don't think there are any secret rooms, Tim," I said.

"But you can't be sure..." Tim began to tap his way along the wall, his eyes half-closed, listening for a hollow sound. A few moments later, he straightened up, excited. "There's definitely something on the other side here!" he cried.

"I know, Tim," I said. "That's the window."

I left him in the bedroom, drying his hair, and went back downstairs. I was going to join the others in the dining-room. But I never got that far. I was about halfway down when I heard it. A short, sudden scream. Then a crashing sound. It had come from somewhere outside.

I ran down the rest of the way, through the hall and out the front door. Mark Tyler appeared, running round the side of the house.

"What was it...?" he demanded. He was trying not to sound scared but it wasn't working.

"Round the back?"

We went there together, moving more slowly now, knowing what we were going to find, not wanting to find it. The kitchen door opened and Brenda Blake came out. I noticed she was breathing heavily.

This time it was Libby Goldman. I'm afraid she had recorded her last episode of *Libby's Lounge* and for her the final credits were already rolling. Why had she gone outside? Maybe she'd decided to light up one of her cigarettes – in which case, this was one time when smoking certainly had been bad for her health. Fatal, in fact. But it hadn't been the tobacco that had killed her. Something had hit her hard on the head: something that had been dropped from above. I looked up, working out the angles. We were directly underneath the battlements. Behind them, the roof was flat. It would have been easy enough for someone to hide up there, to wait for any one of us to step outside. Libby must have come out to get a breath of fresh air before the meeting. Air wasn't something she'd be needing again.

There were footsteps on the gravel. Eric and Tim had arrived. They stared in silence. Mark stretched out a finger and pointed. It took me a minute to work out what he was pointing at. That was how much his finger was trembling.

And there it was, lying in the grass. At first I didn't recognize the object that had been dropped from the roof and which had fallen right onto Libby Goldman. I mean, I knew what it was – but I couldn't believe that that was what had been used.

It was a big round ball: a globe. The sort of thing you find in a library. Maybe it had been in Rory's library before the killer had carried it up to the roof. The United States of America was facing up. It was stained red.

I looked at Eric Draper. His mouth had dropped open. He looked genuinely shocked. Mark Tyler was standing opposite him, staring. Brenda Blake was to one side. She was crying.

One of them had to be faking it. I was certain of it. One of them had to have climbed down from the room after watching Libby fall. There was nobody else here. One of them had to be the killer.

But which one?

MORE MURDER

Eric Draper? Brenda Blake? Or Mark Tyler?

It was early evening and Tim and I had gone for a walk – supposedly to clear our heads. But the truth was, I wanted to be alone with him and somehow I felt safer away from the house. It struck me that all the deaths had taken place inside or near the building. And if we stayed too close to the house something else might strike me – a falling piano or a model of the Taj Mahal, for example.

I glanced down at the piece of paper I was holding in my hand. I had made a few notes just before we left:

RORY McDOUGAL – Killed with a sword.
SYLVIE BINNS – Poisoned.
JANET RHODES – Stabbed with an Eiffel Tower!

LIBBY GOLDMAN – Knocked down with a globe.

There was a pattern in there somewhere but I just couldn't see it. Maybe some fresh air would help after all.

"I've got an idea!" Tim said.

"Go ahead, Tim," I said.

"Maybe I could swim back over to the coast and get some help."

We were sitting on the jetty. Today the sea was flat, the waves caught as if in a photograph. I could just make out the mainland, a vague ribbon lying on the horizon. The sun was setting fast. How many of us would see it rise again?

I shook my head. "No, Tim. It's too far."

"It can't be more than five miles."

"And you can't swim."

"Oh yes. I'd forgotten." He glanced at me. "But you can."

"I can't swim five miles!" I said. "The water's too cold. And there's too much of it. No. Our only hope is to solve this before the killer strikes again."

"You're right, Nick." Tim closed his eyes and sat in silence for a minute. Then he opened them again. "Maybe we could get one of the others to swim…"

"One of the others *is* the killer!" I said. "I saw someone out on the terrace, wearing a skeleton mask. I don't know how they managed to disappear so quickly – but I wasn't imagining it. Brenda saw them too."

"Maybe it was Mark! He's a fast mover."

"And just now … when Libby Goldman was killed. Someone must have climbed up onto the roof." I thought back. "Brenda was out of breath when she came into the garden…"

"She could have been singing!"

"I doubt it. But she could have been running. She drops the globe, then runs all the way downstairs…"

A seagull flew overhead, crying mournfully. I knew how it felt. I almost wanted to cry myself.

"What's missing is the motive," I went on. "Think back, Tim. You were at school with these people. There are only three of them left – Brenda, Mark and Eric. Would any of them have any reason to kill the rest of you?"

Tim sighed. "The only people who ever threatened to kill me," he said, "were the teachers. My French teacher once threw a piece of chalk at me. And when that missed, he threw the blackboard."

"How did you get on with Mark Tyler?"

"We were friends. We used to play conkers together." He scratched his head. "I did once miss his conker and break three of his fingers, but I don't think he minded too much."

"How about Brenda Blake?"

Tim thought back. "She was in the school choir," he said. "She was also in the rugby team. She used to sing in the scrum." He scratched his head. "We used to tease her a bit but it was never serious."

"Maybe she didn't agree."

The waves rolled in towards us. I looked out at the mainland, hoping to catch sight of Horatio Randle and his boat, the *Silver Medal*. But the sea was empty, darkening as the sun dipped behind it. What had the old fisherman said when he'd dropped us? *"I'll be back in a couple of days."* It had been Wednesday when we arrived. He might not return until the weekend. How many passengers would there be left waiting for him?

"How about Eric Draper?" I asked.

"What about him?"

"He could be the killer. It would have to be someone strong to carry the globe up to the roof in the first place. Can you remember anything about him?"

Tim laughed. "He was a great sport. I'll never forget the last day of term when the seven of us pulled off his trousers and threw him in the canal!"

"What?" I exclaimed. "You pulled off his trousers and threw him in the canal? Why?"

"Well, he was the head boy. And he'd always been bossy. It was just a bit of fun. Except that he nearly drowned. And the canal was so polluted, he had to spend six months in hospital."

"Are you telling me that the seven of you nearly killed Eric?" I was almost screaming. "Hasn't it occurred to you that this whole thing could be his revenge?"

"But it was just a joke!"

"You almost killed him, Tim! Maybe he wasn't amused."

I stood up. It was time to go back to the house. The other three would be waiting for us … if they'd managed to survive the last half-hour.

"I wish I'd never come here," Tim muttered.

"I wish you'd never come here," I agreed.

"Poor Libby. And Sylvie. And Janet. And Rory, of course. He was first."

We walked a few more steps in silence. Then I suddenly stopped. "What did you say, Tim?" I demanded.

"I didn't say anything!"

"Yes, you did! Before you weren't saying anything, you were saying something."

"I asked which side of the bed you wanted."

"No. That was yesterday." I played back what he had just said and that was when I saw it, the pattern I'd been looking for. "You're brilliant!" I said.

"Thanks!" Tim frowned. "What have I done?"

"Tell me," I said. "Did Libby come first

in anything at school? And was it ... by any chance ... geography?"

"Yes. She did. How did you know?"

"Let's get back inside," I said.

I found Eric, Mark and Brenda in the drawing-room. This was one of the most extraordinary rooms in the house – almost like a chapel with a great stained glass window at one end and a high, vaulted ceiling. Rory McDougal had obviously fancied himself as a musician. There was even a church organ against the wall, the silver pipes looming over us. Like so many of the other rooms, the walls were lined with old weapons. In here they were antique pistols; muskets and flintlocks. All in all, we couldn't have chosen a worse house to share with a mass murderer. There were more weapons than you'd find in the Tower of London and I just hoped that they weren't as real as they looked.

The three survivors were sitting in heavy, leather chairs. I stood in front of them with the organ on one side and a row of bookshelves on the other. Everyone was watching me and I felt a bit like Hercule Poirot at the end of one of his cases, explaining it to the suspects. The only trouble was, this wasn't the end of the case. I was still certain that I was talking to the murderer. He or she had to be one of the people in the room.

Somewhere outside, a clock chimed the

hour. It was nine o'clock. Night had fallen.

"Seven of you were invited to Crocodile Island," I began. "And I see now that you all have something in common."

"We went to the same school," interrupted Tim.

"I know that, Tim. But there's something else. You all got prizes for coming first. You've already told me that Rory was first in maths. Libby was first in geography..."

"What's this got to do with anything?" Eric snapped.

"Don't you see? Libby was first in geography and someone dropped a globe on her head. Someone told me that Sylvie Binns came first in chemistry and we think she was poisoned."

"Janet came first in French..." Mark murmured.

"...which would explain why she was stabbed with a model of the Eiffel Tower. And Rory McDougal came first in maths."

"He was stabbed too," Eric said.

"He was more than stabbed. He was divided!"

There was a long silence.

"That's the reason why Johnny Nadler wasn't invited to the island," Brenda said. "He never came first in anything. He was second..."

"But that means..." Eric had gone pale. "I came first in history."

"I came first in sport," Mark said.

Brenda nodded. "And I came first in music."

We all turned to look at Tim. But he couldn't have come first in anything ... could he? I noticed he was blushing. He licked his lips and looked the other way.

"What did you come first in, Tim?" I asked.

"I didn't..." he began, but I could tell he was lying.

"We have to know," I said. "It could be important."

"I remember..." Brenda began.

"All right," Tim sighed. "I got first prize in needlework."

"Needlework!" I exclaimed.

"Well ... yes. It was a hobby of mine. Just for a bit. I mean..." He was going redder and redder. "I didn't even want the prize. I just got it. It was for a handkerchief..."

The idea of my sixteen-year-old brother winning a prize for an embroidered hanky made my head spin. But this wasn't the time to laugh. Hopefully I'd be able to do that later.

"Wait a minute! Wait a minute!" Eric said. He looked annoyed. Maybe it was because I was ten years younger than him and I was the one who'd worked it out. "I came first in history – and you're saying I'm going to be killed ... *historically*?"

"That's what it looks like," I said.

"But how...?"

I pointed at the wall, at the flintlock pistols on the wooden plaques. "Maybe someone will use one of those," I said. "Or there are swords, arrows, spears … that bear upstairs is even holding a blunderbuss. This place is full of old weapons."

"What about me?" Brenda whispered.

"You're not an old weapon!" Tim said.

"I came first in music." Brenda glared at the organ as if it was about to jump off the wall and eat her.

"But who's *doing* this?" Mark cut in. "I mean … it's got to be someone in this room. Right? We know there's nobody else on the island. There can't be anybody hiding. We've searched everywhere."

"It's him!" Brenda pointed at Eric. "He never forgave us for throwing him in the canal. This is his revenge!"

"What about *you*?" Eric returned. "You once said you were going to kill us all. It was in the school yard. I remember it clearly!"

"That's true!" Mark said.

"You used to bully me all the time," Brenda wailed. "Just because I had pigtails. And crooked teeth."

"And you were fat," Tim reminded her.

"But I didn't mean it, when I said that." She turned to Mark. "You said you were going to kill Tim when he broke all your fingers with that conker!"

"I only broke three of them!" Tim interrupted.

"I didn't much like Tim," Mark agreed. "And you're right. I would have quite happily strangled him. Not that it would have been easy with three broken fingers. But I never had any argument with you or with Eric or any of the others. Why would I want to kill you?"

"It's still got to be one of us," Eric insisted. He paused. "It can't be Tim," he went on.

"Why not?" Tim asked.

"Because this whole business is the work of a fiendish madman and you're not fiendish. You're just silly!"

"Oh thanks!" Tim looked away.

"I know it's not me..." Eric went on.

"That's what you say," Brenda sniffed.

"I know it's not me, so it's got to be Brenda or Mark."

"What about Sylvie?" Tim suggested.

"She's already dead, Tim," I reminded him, quietly.

"Oh yes."

"This is all irrelevant," Mark said. "The question is – what are we going to do? We could be stuck on this island for days, or even weeks. It all depends on when Captain Randle comes back. And by then it could be too late!"

"I'd like to make a suggestion," I said. Everyone stopped and looked at me. "The first thing is, we've all got to keep each other in sight."

"The kid's right," Mark agreed. "So long as we can see each other, we're going to be safe."

"That's true!" Tim exclaimed. "All we have to do is keep our eyes open and everything will be fine." He turned to me. "You're brilliant, Nick. For a moment there I was getting really worried."

Then all the lights went out.

It happened so suddenly that for a moment I thought it was just me. Had I been knocked out or somehow closed my eyes without noticing? The last thing I saw was the four of them – Eric, Brenda, Mark and Tim – sitting in their chairs as if caught in a photograph. Then everything was black. There was no moon that night and even if there had been the stained glass window would have kept most of the light out. Darkness came crashing onto us. It was total.

"Don't panic!" Eric said.

There was a gunshot. I saw it, a spark of red on the other side of the room.

Tim screamed and for a horrible moment I wondered if he had been shot. I forced myself to calm down. He'd come first in needlework. Nobody would be aiming a gun at him.

"Tim!" I called out.

"Can I panic now?" he called back.

"Eric...?" That was Mark's voice.

And then there was a sort of groaning sound, followed by a heavy thud. At the same time I heard a door open and close. I stood up, trying to see through the darkness. But it was hopeless. I couldn't even make out my own hand in front of my face.

"Tim?" I called again.

"Nick?" I was relieved to hear his voice.

"Eric?" I tried.

Silence.

"Brenda?"

Nothing.

"Mark?"

The lights came back on.

There were only two people alive in the room. I was standing in front of my chair. One more step and I'd have put my foot through the coffee table. Tim was *under* the coffee table. He must have crawled there when the lights went out. Eric was on the floor. He had been shot. There was a flintlock pistol, still smoking, lying on the carpet on the other side of the room. It must have been taken off the wall, fired and then dropped. At least, that's what it looked like. Brenda was sitting in her chair. She was dead too. One of the organ pipes – the largest – had been pulled down on top of her. That must have been the thud I had heard. Brenda had sung her last opera. The only music she needed now was a hymn.

There was no sign of Mark.

"Are you all right, Tim?" I demanded.

"Yes!" Tim sounded surprised. "I haven't been murdered!" he exclaimed.

"I noticed." I waited while he climbed out from underneath the coffee table. "At least we know who the killer is," I said.

"Do we?"

"It's got to be Mark," I said. "Mark Tyler…"

"I always knew it was him," Tim said. "Call it intuition. Call it experience. But I knew he was a killer even before he'd done any killing."

"I don't know, Tim," I said. It bothered me, because to be honest Mark was the last person I would have suspected. And yet, at the same time, I had to admit … it would have taken a fast mover to push the globe off the roof and make it all the way downstairs in time and Mark was the fastest person on the island.

"Where do you think he went?" Tim asked.

"I don't know."

We left the room carefully. In fact, Tim made me leave it first. The fact was that – unless I'd got the whole thing wrong – it was just the three of us now on the island; Mark could be waiting for us anywhere. Or waiting for Tim, rather. He had no quarrel with me. And that made me think. Tim had come first in needlework. Following the pattern of the other deaths, that meant he would probably

148

be killed with some sort of needle. But what would that mean? A sewing needle dipped in poison? A hypodermic syringe?

Tim must have had the same thought. He was looking everywhere, afraid to touch anything, afraid even to take another step. We went out into the hall. The fire had died down and was glowing red. The front door was open.

"Maybe he went outside," Tim said.

"What would be the point?" I asked.

Tim shuddered. "Don't talk about points," he said.

We went outside. And that was where we found Mark. He had come first in sport but now he had reached the finishing line. Somebody had been throwing the javelin and they'd thrown it at him. It had hit him in the chest. He was lying on the grass, doing a good impersonation of a sausage on a stick.

"It's … it's … it's…" Tim couldn't finish the sentence.

"Yeah," I said. "It's Mark." There were a few leaves scattered around his body. That puzzled me. The nearest trees were ten metres away. But this wasn't the time to play the detective. There were no more suspects. And only one more victim.

I looked at Tim.

Tim looked at me.

We were the only two left.

NEEDLES

Tim didn't sleep well that night. Although I hadn't said anything, not wanting to upset him, even he had managed to work out that he had to be the next on the killer's list. He also knew that his own murder would have something to do with needlework. So he was looking for needles everywhere.

By one o'clock in the morning we knew that there were no sewing needles in the room, no knitting needles and no pine needles. Even so, it took him an hour to get into bed and several more hours to get to sleep. Mind you, nobody would have found it easy getting to sleep dressed in a full suit of medieval armour, but that still hadn't stopped Tim putting it on.

"There could be a poisoned needle in the mattress," he said. "Or someone could try and inject me with a syringe."

Tim didn't snore that night; he clanked.

Every time he rolled over he sounded like twenty cans of beans in a washing machine. I just hoped he wasn't planning to take a bath in the suit of armour the following morning. That way he could end up rusting to death.

At four-thirty, he woke up screaming.

"What is it, Tim?" I asked.

"I had a bad dream, Nick," he said.

"Don't tell me. You saw a needle."

"No. I saw a haystack."

I didn't sleep well either. I got cramp and woke up in the morning with pins and needles. I didn't tell Tim, though. He'd have had a fit.

We had breakfast together in the kitchen. Neither of us ate very much. For a start, we were surrounded by dead bodies, which didn't make us feel exactly cheerful. But Tim was also terrified. I'd managed to persuade him to change out of the armour but now he was worrying about the food. Were there going to be needles in the cereal? A needle in the tea? In the end, I gave him a straw with a tissue sellotaped over the end. The tissue worked as a filter and he was able to suck up a little orange juice and a very softly-boiled egg.

I have to say that for once I was baffled. It was still like being in an Agatha Christie novel – only this time I couldn't flick through to the last page and see who did it without bothering to read the rest. Personally, I had always thought Eric had been the killer. He seemed to have the strongest motive – being half-drowned on the last day of school. It was funny really. All eight of the old boys and girls of St Egbert's had disliked each other. But someone, somewhere, had disliked them all even more. The whole thing had been planned right down to the last detail. And the last detail, unfortunately, was Tim.

But who? And why?

Tim sat miserably at his end of the table, hardly daring to move. Why had he had to come first in *needlework* of all things? How was I supposed to find the needle that was going to kill him? I knew now that the only hope for me was to solve this thing before the killer struck one last time. And a nasty thought had already occurred to me. Would the killer stop with Tim? I wasn't meant to be part of this. I had never gone to St Egbert's. But I was a witness to what had happened and maybe I had seen too much.

I went over what had happened last night. We had always assumed that there was nobody else on the island, but thinking it through I knew this couldn't be true. We had all been sitting down: Brenda in front of the organ, Eric opposite her, Mark nearest the door and Tim and me on the sofa. But none of us had been anywhere near the light switch, and someone had most certainly turned off the lights – not just in the drawing-room but throughout the entire house. Somewhere down in the basement, there would be a main fuse switch. But that led to another question. If the killer had been down in the basement, then how had he or she managed to appear in the room seconds later to shoot Eric and push the organ pipe onto Brenda?

At the time, I had assumed that Mark had committed the last two murders. There had been a shot, then a thud, then the opening and closing of a door. But a few seconds later, Mark had himself been killed. And what about the leaves that I had seen lying next to his body? How had they got there?

I thought back to the other murders. Rory first. We had all been on the island and we had all separated. Any one of us could have attacked him and, immediately afterwards, left the chocolate on the bed for Sylvie to find. That was the night I had seen the face at the window. A face that had appeared and disappeared – impossibly – in seconds. And then we had found Janet. I remembered her lying in her bed, stabbed by a model of the Eiffel Tower. Her room had been shabby. There had been a tear in the canopy ... I had remarked on it at the time. Why had it caught my eye?

Libby Goldman next. The television presenter had been knocked down with a model globe. There was something strange about that, too. Someone must have carried it up to the roof and dropped it on her when she came out of the front door. But now that I thought about it, I hadn't seen the globe in any of the rooms when we had been searching the house. And that could only mean one thing. It had been on the roof from the very start, waiting for her...

Maybe you know how it is when you've been given a particularly nasty piece of homework – an impossible equation or a fiendish bit of physics or something. You stare at it and stare at it, but it's all just ink on paper and you're about to give up when you notice something and suddenly you realize it's not so difficult after all. Well, that was what was happening to me now.

I remembered the search party, slowly criss-crossing the island. We had seen security cameras everywhere and from the day I had arrived, I had felt that I was being watched. There was a security camera in the kitchen. I looked up. It was watching me even now. Were there cameras in other rooms, too?

At the same time, I remembered something Mark had said, when we had found the old photograph of St Egbert's. And in that second, as quickly as that, I suddenly knew everything.

"I've got it, Tim!" I said.

"So have I, Nick!" Tim cried.

I'd been so wrapped up in my own thoughts, that I hadn't noticed Tim had been thinking too. Now he was staring at me with the sort of look you see on a fish when it's spent too long out of water.

"You know who did it?" I asked.

"Yes."

"Go on!"

"It's simple!" Tim explained. "First there were eight of us on the island, then seven, then six, then five..."

"I know," I interrupted. "I can count backwards."

"Well, now there are only two of us left. I know it wasn't me who committed the murders." He reached forward and snatched up a spoon. Then he realized what he'd done, put it down and snatched up a knife. He waved it at me. "So the killer must be you!" he exclaimed.

"What?" I couldn't believe what I was hearing.

"There's only us left. You and me. I know it wasn't me so it must have been you."

"But why would I want to kill everyone?" I demanded.

"You tell me!"

"I wouldn't! And I didn't! Don't be ridiculous, Tim."

I stood up. That was a mistake.

"Don't come near me!" Tim yelled, and suddenly he sprang out of his chair and jumped out of the window. This was an impressive feat. The window wasn't even open.

I couldn't believe what had happened. I knew Tim was stupid but this was remarkable even by his standards. Maybe sleeping in a suit of armour had done something to that tiny organism he called his brain. At the same time, I was suddenly worried. I knew who the killer was now and I knew who was lined up to be the next victim. Tim was outside the house, on his own. He had made himself into a perfect target.

I had no choice. I went after him, jumping through the shattered window. I could see Tim a short distance away, running towards the tail of Crocodile Island. I had no idea where he was going. But nor of course did he. He was panicking – just trying to put as much distance between the two of us as he could. Not easy considering he was trapped on a small island.

"Tim!" I called.

He didn't stop. I ran after him, following the path as it began to climb steeply up towards the cliffs. This was where the island tapered to a point. I slowed down. Tim had already reached the far end. He had nowhere else to go.

The wind blew his hair around his head as he turned to face me. He was still holding the knife. I noticed now that it was a butter knife. If he stabbed me with all his strength he might just manage to give me a small bruise. His face was pale and his eyes were wide open and staring. The last time I had seen him like this was when they had shown *Jurassic Park* on TV.

"Get back, Nick!" he yelled. It was hard to hear him above the crash of the waves.

"You're crazy, Tim!" I called back. "Why would I want to hurt you? I'm your brother. Think about all the adventures we've had together! I've saved your life lots of times." I thought of telling him that I loved him but he'd have known that wasn't true. "I quite like you!" I said. "You've looked after me ever since Mum and Dad emigrated to Australia. We've had fun together!"

Tim hesitated. I could see the doubt in his eyes. He lowered the butter knife. A huge wave rolled in and crashed against the rocks, spraying us both with freezing, salt water. I looked past Tim at the rocks, an idea forming in my mind. There were six iron grey rocks, jutting out of the sea. I had noticed them the day we had searched the island. And of course, rocks like that have a name. Long and slender with pointed tops, standing upright in the water...

They're called needles.

I'm not exactly sure what happened next but I do know that it all happened at the same time.

There was a soft explosion, just where Tim was standing. The earth underneath his feet seemed to separate, falling away.

Tim screamed and his arm jerked. The butter knife spun in the air, the sun glinting off the blade.

I yelled out and threw myself forward. Somehow my hands managed to grab hold of Tim's shirt.

"Don't kill me!" Tim whimpered.

"I'm not killing you, you idiot!" I yelled. "I'm saving you!"

We rolled back together, away from the edge of the cliff ... an edge that was now several centimetres closer to us than it had been seconds before. I was dazed and there was grass in my mouth, but I realized that the killer had struck again. There had been a small explosive charge buried in the ground at the end of the cliff. Someone had detonated it and if I hadn't managed to grab hold of Tim, he would have fallen down towards to the sea, only to crash onto the needles fifty metres below.

We lay on the grass, panting. The sun was beating down on us. It was difficult to see. But then I became aware of a shadow moving towards us. I rolled over and looked up at the figure, limping towards us, a radio transmitter in one hand and a gun in the other.

"Well, well, well," he said. "It looks as if my little plan has finally come unstuck. And just when everything was going so well, too!"

Tim stared at the man. At his single eye,

his single leg, his huge beard. "It's ... it's..." he began.

"It's Horatio Randle," I said. "Captain of the *Silver Medal,* the boat that brought us here."

"You got it in one, young lad!" he said.

"But that's not his real name," I went on. "Randle is an anagram. If you switch around the letters, you get..."

"Endral!" Tim exclaimed.

"Nadler," I said. "I think this must be Johnny Nadler. Your old school friend from St Egbert's."

The captain put down the radio transmitter. He had used it, of course, to set off the explosive charge a few moments before. He didn't let go of the gun. With his free hand, he reached up and pulled off the fake beard, the wig and the eye patch. At the same time, he twisted round and released the leg that he'd had tied up behind his back. It only took a few seconds but at once I recognized the thin-faced teenager I had seen in the photograph.

"It seems you've worked it all out," he muttered. His accent had changed too. He was no longer the jolly captain. He was a killer. And he was mad.

"Yes," I said.

"But it's impossible!" Tim burbled. "He couldn't have killed all the others. We looked! There was nobody else on the island!"

"It was Nadler all along," I said. I glanced

at him. The wind raced past and the waves crashed down.

He smiled. "Do go on," he snarled.

"I know what you did," I said. "Last Wednesday, you met us all at the quay, disguised as a captain. You'd sent everyone invitations to this reunion on the island and you even offered to pay a thousand pounds to make sure that they'd all come. Rory McDougal had nothing to do with it, of course. You'd killed him before we even set sail."

"That's right," Nadler said. He was smiling now. There was something horrible about that smile. He was sure this was one story I wouldn't be telling anyone else.

"You killed Rory and you left the poisoned chocolate for Sylvie. Then you dropped us on the island and sailed away again. There was no need for you to stay. Everything was already prepared."

"Are you saying ... he wasn't here when he killed everyone?" Tim asked. He was still lying on the grass. There was a buttercup lodged behind his ear.

"That's right. Don't you remember what Mark told us when we were looking at the picture? He said that Johnny Nadler wanted to be an inventor when he left school. He said he was always playing with planes and cars." I glanced at the transmitter lying on the ground just a few feet away. "I assume they were radio-controlled planes and cars," I said.

"That's right!" Tim said. "He was brilliant, Nick! He once landed a helicopter on the science teacher's head!"

"Well, that's how he killed everyone on the island – after he'd finished with Rory McDougal and Sylvie Binns." I took a deep breath, wondering if there was anything I could do. Tim was right next to the edge of the cliff. I was a couple of metres in front of him. We were both lying down. Nadler was standing over us, aiming with the gun. If we so much as moved, he could shoot us both. I had to keep talking and hope that I might somehow find a way to distract him.

"Janet Rhodes was stabbed with an Eiffel Tower," I went on. "But I noticed that there was a tear in the canopy above her bed. I should have put two and two together and realized that the Eiffel Tower was always there, above the bed. It must have been mounted on some sort of spring mechanism. Nadler knew that was where she'd be sleeping. All he had to do was press a button and send the model plunging down. He was probably miles away when he killed her."

"That's right!" Nadler giggled. "I was back on the mainland. I was nowhere near!"

"But what about the face you saw?" Tim asked. "The skull at the window! Brenda saw it too!"

"You've already answered that one, Tim," I said. "A remote control helicopter or something with a mask hanging underneath. Nadler controlled that too. It was easy!"

"But how could he see us?"

I glanced at Nadler and he nodded. He was happy for me to explain how it had been done.

"The whole island is covered in cameras," I said. "That was Rory's security system. We've been watched from the moment we arrived. Nadler knew where we were every minute of the day."

"Right again!" Nadler grinned. He was pleased with himself, I could see that. "It was easy to hack into McDougal's security system and redirect the pictures to my own TV monitor. I was even able to watch you in the bath!"

"That's outrageous!" Tim was blushing. He knew that Nadler would have seen him playing with his plastic duck.

"Nadler had positioned the globe up on the roof," I went on. "If we'd gone up and looked we'd probably have found some sort of ramp with a simple switch. He waited until Libby Goldman came out of the front door and then he pressed the button that released the globe. It rolled forward and that was that. She never had a chance. He killed Eric and Brenda the same way. First he turned out the lights. Then he fired a bullet and brought down an organ pipe ... both by remote control." I paused.

"How about Mark Tyler?" I asked.

"The javelin was hidden in the branches of a tree," Nadler explained. "It was on a giant elastic band. Remote control again. It was just like a crossbow." He giggled for a second time. "Only bigger."

Well that explained the leaves. Some of them must have travelled with the javelin when it was fired.

"And that just left you, Tim," I said. "Nadler had to wait until you came out here. Then he was going to blow the ground out from beneath your feet and watch you fall onto the needles below. And with you dead, his revenge would be complete."

"Revenge?" Tim was genuinely puzzled. "But why did he want revenge? We never did anything to him!"

"I think it was because he came second," I said. I turned to Nadler. "You came second in every subject at school. And the boat you picked us up in. It was called the *Silver Medal*. I guess you chose the name on purpose. Because that's what you're given when you come second."

"That's right." Nadler nodded and now his face had darkened and his lips were twisted into an expression of pain. His finger tightened on the trigger and he looked at me with hatred in his eyes. "I came second in maths, second in chemistry, second in French, second in

163

geography, second in history, second in music and second in sport. I even came second in needlework, even though my embroidered tea towel was much more beautiful than your brother's stupid handkerchief!"

"It was a lovely handkerchief!" Tim said.

"Shut up!" Nadler screamed and for a moment I was afraid he was going to shoot Tim then and there. "Do you have any idea how horrible it is coming second?" he went on. Saliva flecked at his lips. The hand with the gun never moved. "Coming last doesn't matter. Coming fifth or sixth ... who cares? But when you come second, everyone knows. You've just missed! You've missed getting the prize by just a few marks. And everyone feels sorry for you. Poor old Johnny! He couldn't quite make it. He wasn't quite good enough."

He took a deep breath. "I've been coming second all my life. I go for jobs and I get down to the last two in the interviews but it's always the other person who gets it. I went out with a girl but then she decided to marry someone else because as far as she was concerned, I was Number Two. When I've tried to sell my inventions, I've discovered that someone else has always got there first. Number Two! Number Two! Number Two! I hate being Number Two...!

"And it's all your fault!" He pointed the gun at Tim and now the fury was back in his eyes. "It all started at St Egbert's! That hateful school! That was where I started coming second and that was why I decided to have my revenge. You all thought you were clever beating me at everything. Well, I've showed you! I've killed the whole lot of you and I've done it in exactly the way you deserve!"

"You haven't killed me!" Tim exclaimed.

I didn't think it was a good idea to point this out. Nadler steadied the gun. "I'm going to do that now," he said. "Your body will still end up smashing into the needles so everything will have worked out the way it was meant to." He nodded at me. "I'll have to kill you too, of course," he continued. "You weren't meant to be here, but I don't mind. You sound too clever for your own good. I'm going to enjoy killing you too!"

He took aim.

"No!" I shouted.

He fired at Tim.

"Missed!" Tim laughed and rolled to one side. He was still laughing when he rolled over the side of the cliff.

"Tim!" I yelled.

"Now it's your turn," Nadler said.

I closed my eyes. There was nothing I could do.

There was a long pause. I opened them again.

Nadler was still standing, but even as I watched he crumpled to the ground. Eric

Draper, the fat solicitor, was standing behind him. There was blood all over his shirt and he was deathly pale. But he was still alive. He was holding the blunderbuss, which he must have taken from the bear. He hadn't fired it. He had used it like a club and knocked Nadler out.

"He only wounded me..." he gasped. "I woke up this morning. I came to find you..."

But I wasn't interested in Eric Draper, even if he had just saved my life. I crawled over to the cliff edge and looked down, expecting to see Tim, smashed to pieces, on the rocks below.

"Hello, Nick!" Tim said.

There was a gorse bush growing out of the side of the cliff. He had fallen right onto it. I held out a hand. Tim took it. I pulled him to safety and we both lay there in the sun, exhausted, glad to be alive.

We found the *Silver Medal* moored at the jetty and I steered it back towards the mainland. Eric was slumped on the deck. Johnny Nadler was down below, tied up with so much rope that only his head was showing. We weren't taking any chances after what had happened. We had already radioed ahead to the police. They would be waiting when we got to the mainland. Tim was standing next to me. We had left six dead bodies behind us on Crocodile

Island. Well, I warned you that it was going to be a horror story.

"I'm sorry I thought you were the killer," Tim said. He was looking even more sheepish than ... well, a sheep.

"It's all right, Tim," I said. "It's a mistake anyone could have made." He swayed on his feet and suddenly I felt sorry for him. "Do you want to sit down?" I asked. "It's going to take us a while to get back."

Tim shook his head. "No." He blushed. "I can't!"

"Why not?"

"That bush I fell into. It was very prickly. My bottom's full of..."

"What?"

"...needles!"

I pushed down on the throttle and the boat surged forward. Behind us, Crocodile Island shimmered in the morning mist until at last it had disappeared.

READ OTHER GREAT BOOKS BY
ANTHONY HOROWITZ...

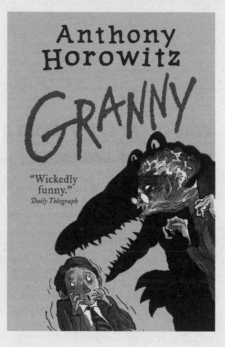

Joe Warden isn't happy. He has rich, uncaring
parents and he's virtually a prisoner in the huge
family mansion, Thattlebee Hall. But his real
problem is his granny. Not only is she physically
repulsive and unbelievably mean, she seems to have
some secret plan – and that plan involves him.

Can Joe thwart Granny's evil scheme before he's
turned into neoplasmic slime?

"Wickedly funny." *Daily Telegraph*

"Hugely popular ... I can hear Horowitz fans
drooling." *The Times*

COLLECT ALL OF THE HILARIOUS DIAMOND BROTHERS INVESTIGATIONS

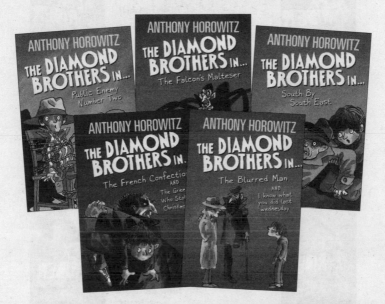

Tim Diamond is the world's worst private detective, and unfortunately for his quick-thinking brother, Nick, the cases keep coming in. What connects them? Murder! And if the Diamond Brothers don't play their cards right, they could be next!

"Horowitz is the perfect writer.
His dialogue crackles with hardboiled wit."
Frank Cottrell Boyce, *Guardian*

Collect all the Alex Rider books

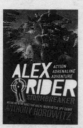

STORMBREAKER

Alex Rider – you're never too young to die…

POINT BLANC

High in the Alps, death waits for Alex Rider…

SKELETON KEY

Sharks. Assassins. Nuclear bombs. Alex Rider's in deep water.

EAGLE STRIKE

Alex Rider has 90 minutes to save the world.

SCORPIA

Once stung, twice as deadly. Alex Rider wants revenge.

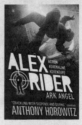

ARK ANGEL

He's back – and this time there are no limits.

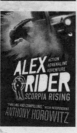

SNAKEHEAD

Alex Rider bites back…

CROCODILE TEARS

Alex Rider – in the jaws of death…

SCORPIA RISING

One bullet. One life. The end starts here.

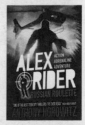

RUSSIAN ROULETTE

Get your hands on the deadly prequel

www.alexrider.com

WELCOME TO THE DARK SIDE OF ANTHONY HOROWITZ

THE POWER OF FIVE

BOOK ONE

He always knew he was different.
First there were the dreams.
Then the deaths began.

BOOK TWO

It began with Raven's Gate.
But it's not over yet. Once
again the enemy is stirring.

BOOK THREE

Darkness covers the earth.
The Old Ones have returned.
The battle must begin.

BOOK FOUR

An ancient evil is unleashed.
Five have the power to defeat it.
But one of them has been taken.

BOOK FIVE

Five Gatekeepers.
One chance to save mankind.
Chaos beckons. Oblivion awaits.

Photograph © Jon Cartwright

Anthony Horowitz is the author of the number one bestselling Alex Rider books and The Power of Five series. He has enjoyed huge success as a writer for both children and adults, most recently with the latest adventure in the Alex Rider series, *Russian Roulette*, and the highly acclaimed Sherlock Holmes novel, *The House of Silk*. His latest novel, *Moriarty*, is also set in the world of Sherlock Holmes and was published in October 2014. Anthony was also chosen by the Ian Fleming estate to write the new James Bond novel which will be published this year. Anthony has won numerous awards, including the Bookseller Association/Nielsen Author of the Year Award, the Children's Book of the Year Award at the British Book Awards, and the Red House Children's Book Award. In 2014 Anthony was awarded an OBE for Services to Literature. He has also created and written many major television series, including *Injustice*, *Collision* and the award-winning *Foyle's War*.

You can find out more about Anthony and his work at:
www.alexrider.com
@AnthonyHorowitz